Chess with Carrizo

J.W. Stephens, Author

The Chihuahua Desert

A raised eyebrow greeted Chris as he ducked his head past the doorway and quickly looked around the tiny room. He entered the room in a half crouch, his light blue eyes searching the dim space for any movement other than the woman with the arched brow. A 4 inch Condor Bushlore knife was held lightly in his right hand, and a two foot, round piece of steel in the left hand, both dripping fresh blood on the dirt floor. His blonde hair was cut short, at odds with the beard on his face. Chris's blue jeans were covered in a layer of brown dust, his cowboy boots tracked bloody footprints with every step as he approached the woman.

Tru cleared her throat impatiently as she watched Chris make his way closer to her. The duct tape over her mouth prevented actual words. More duct tape bound her wrists behind her back and her ankles were similarly tied in front of her. She was seated with her back against the stucco wall, facing the doorway. She rolled onto her left side and waggled her bound hands at him. Her thick red hair was caught in a disheveled pony tail, her clothes were filthy and damp with sweat. Tru had a shiner starting over the left eye and a cut on her cheekbone below it. Not her best look to be sure, but then again, it had not been a great day all the way around.

Chris stared hard at her face, his rage glimmering off him like a wave of heat. Dropping the pipe, he took her chin between his fingers, turning her head from side to side. Tru waggled her arms again, jerking both eyebrows up and down pointedly at the same time. "Sorry" he muttered and promptly started cutting the tape from her wrists with the bloody knife. As she stretched the cramps out of her fingers and gingerly rolled her shoulders forward, she cleared her throat loudly, looking him in the eye. Chris sighed deeply and gently pulled the tape from her mouth.

"Where the HELL have you been? Piddle around much?" Tru's tone was light, teasing almost. Chris did not look up as he started slicing at the duct tape on her ankles. "You do understand why a man would be tempted to leave your mouth gagged, right?" he calmly asked. ""Ready to go?" Once her ankles were free, he darted back to the doorway, motioning behind him for her to come on. She stood up slowly, testing her ankles' ability to bear weight properly before she followed Chris.

They stood in silence near the doorway, the moonlight shining on a dead man lying at the threshold, blood pooling alongside his severed throat. Chris turned with his back against the wall and reached behind him to pull a pistol from the small of his back. He handed it butt first to Tru and patted the holster on his hip to reassure that his own weapon was where he could get to it. "Thank you!" Tru smiled at him as she chambered a round in the Glock 45 caliber pistol and balanced it in her right hand. It felt comfortable. It felt right to be armed again.

"Hey. Where is your engagement ring?" Chris nodded to her left hand.

"You find me on the floor, bound and gagged in the middle of nowhere and THAT is what you're worried about?"

"It was an expensive emerald." he grunted, his eyes once again looking out the doorway of the hut.

"Big too. I swallowed it. We'll see it in a couple of days I imagine." Tru was right behind him, staring outside over his shoulder.

"All right honey. Follow me and stay quiet. We leave this hut, turn left for about 100 feet to that big bunch of ocotillo plants. Straight from there about a football field length and you'll see the horses. If we get into a fire fight you RUN. Understand?"

Tru took a deep breath to steady her nerves and then she noticed the grin on Chris' face. He casually stepped over the very fat dead guy in the doorway and into the night beyond.

The night was hot, no breeze moved the heat and the scent of fresh blood hung in the air. Goats could be heard in the distance and a hoot owl further away. No human noises were heard as Tru and Chris edged their way out of the hut and along the side to a path illuminated by moonlight. Tru jumped slightly as the thin metal roof of the hut creaked when a lizard darted over it. Chris didn"t even acknowledge the sound, his eyes darting from side to side as he led his wife through the ramshackle collection of dirt casitas. His immediate goal was to get to the arroyo where he had left their two horses without being shot in the process. Bonus points if he could kill a couple more of the sons of bitches who had snatched her in the first place.

They paused just beyond the perimeter in a group of ocotillo plants and took stock of the situation. Tru's hand was wrapped easily around her Glock. Chris brushed a finger over the line of her jaw and she whispered ""I never doubted you, you know." He just winked at her. She could hear the soft snuffling noises of horses now and she started off in that direction, Chris right behind her, splitting his attention to the path behind them. Watching for pursuers. Watching to see if anyone was still alive who could pursue them. Being a killer did not faze him in the least. His wife or these cartel members? That choice was so simple he gave it no thought at all. Slitting their throats had taken no more emotional toll than buttering a biscuit at his breakfast table. What did worry Chris was not being sure if there were others out there somewhere who would want payback. They had a 36 hour ride through the harsh terrain of the Chihuahuan desert back to Texas. Alone they could make it with a minimum of drama, but chased by a Mexican Cartel? Well.... that did present a problem.

Chapter One ~Five Days Earlier

Tru and Chris Marcus had been married eight years and together in some form or fashion a total of fifteen years. Theirs was a happy marriage built on a bedrock of unbreakable friendship. Childless by choice, they spent their time and money on a pack of hound dogs and their horses. Chris was former military special forces and Tru was the love of his life. They ran a small horse training business in South Texas. Periodically Chris would take a consulting contract for private companies, teaching them about hostage negotiations and basic security in hostile environments. They weren't rich, but they could afford to do a little traveling and indulge in a few luxuries.

They had a long standing tradition of spending a few weeks a year in New Orleans and along the Texas-Mexico border in Big Bend country. New Orleans was Tru's city more than Chris, but Big Bend was theirs. Both had a deep love for the wildness, the beauty and fierceness of the land. They would head down to the cabin just southwest of Terlingua whenever the opportunity presented itself. They had purchased 100 acres in the Christmas Mountains with a rustic cabin and an iffy water well. Solar panels provided electricity in a limited capacity for their long weekends. Cell phone service was non existent and a land line was not an option due to the remote location. They had built a small barn with four stalls and fenced paddocks which allowed them to bring a couple of horses on each trip. Most of the places in this part of Texas that Chris and Tru wanted to spend time in were inaccessible except on foot or horseback. Visiting the cabin was more than a little like stepping back in time.

Two small bedrooms, a full bath, a kitchen and family room combo and wrap around porch. The fanciest thing in the entire place was the huge gas generator on the back porch. Chris installed it for those days when the sand storms covered the sky for miles, rendering the solar panels useless. Really though, Tru was the one who made sure they brought 30 gallons of gas every trip so she could run the window unit air conditioners. "Roughing"" it was one thing, being savages with no air conditioning at all was quite another.

The end of October was actually one of the best times of year for West Texas. Still hot, but not the melt you in your boots hot of July and August. They had planned a fall trip to the cabin for their closest friends, Janet and David Burgess and their twin twelve year old boys. They loaded four horses into the trailer for the trip and left the dogs at the kennel. The dogs only went to the cabin when it was just Chris and Tru. It was far too small for six people and six hound dogs at the same time.

This was the first time Janet and David had brought the kids up to the cabin. Chris wanted to make sure the boys got a chance to ride horses, hunt for fossils and shoot while they were there. Just a long weekend with good friends enjoying Mother Nature. Chris also viewed it as a chance to show the twins that not everything involves the internet or Nintendo Wii. Tru and Chris ran down the porch steps to greet them when the Burgess Suburban pulled up.

"My God! Is the road up here that rough on purpose? My whole ass is numb!" David hugged Tru hard as he climbed out of the green Suburban.

Janet laughed out loud as she exited the front passenger seat, countering with "Chris just ignore him. You know these transplanted Yankees... if the deli or coffee shop won't deliver to your door, you must live in the boonies or some circle of Hell."

"Can we see the horses Aunt Tru??" The twins fell out of the back doors at the same time, bouncing up to Tru with big blue eyes and bigger grins. They were identical with close cropped blonde hair and freckles over the bridges of their noses. "Are there wild animals? Snakes? Can we see some snakes Aunt Tru?"

"NO! YOU MAY NOT SEE SNAKES! What the hell is wrong with you guys?" Janet gave a whole body shiver at the very idea of playing with snakes. Chris choked back a laugh and told the boys to head back behind the cabin to the barn if they wanted to see the horses. Janet was still muttering "Snakes... Jesus help me. They are boys, puppy dog tails and all that, but just... Yuck."

"The only snake Janet wants to see is the one on a pair of Italian high heels" David said it with a wink as he shook Chris' hand and they turned to grab the luggage from the back of the truck. It was a comfortable, old friendship and they fell back into familiar rhythms easily.

The first night found everyone sitting out on the porch at midnight watching the Milky Way float past in the crystal clear sky. The boys were half asleep and thus far had not uttered one word about video games or failed cell phone connections. A generous meal of venison steaks, corn on the cob, and au gratin potatoes had left the whole group lethargically patting their bellies. Of course, the black & white cookies from Dean and Deluca were the piece de resistance - leave it to David to schlep two dozen cookies across the entire nation to a cabin in the old West.

Bedtime was a smooth transition with the twins, Todd and Jeff, sleeping on the foldout sofa in the living room. A line of lightening flashed to the west of the cabin as the last lights were put out for the night.

Chapter Two

There were four horses in the Marcus barn, happily chewing hay when Tru introduced Todd and Jeff to them. Two large black mares, each with a white star on their foreheads were in the stalls on the left of the aisle. On the other side of the barn stood a smaller bay mare with a black mane and tail, her head hanging over her stall door waiting for a peppermint. The last stall held a blue roan stallion, smaller than the mares, but far more regal in attitude and slightly disdainful of all the cooing going on in his barn. Tru allowed the boys to give the horses a treat as she explained which horse was whose to ride during their stay.

"Ok boys, the twin black mares are for you guys. I know they are enormous, but don't worry. They are Spanish Normans - half Andalusian and half Percheron draft horse. That means they're surefooted, easy to get along with and smart. These girls will take care of you out in the desert, they won't leave you if you fall off. If you get lost, they can find their way home. The bay mare and the blue horse over here are both Spanish Mustangs which is why they are smaller. They are half Andalusian and half wild mustang." Tru walked to stand by the bay mare.

"Your Mom will be riding Whiskey, and I'll be on Azul." The boys wandered to each stall looking the horses over with serious expressions and then turned to eyeball their Mother. Janet raised an eyebrow and waited. Finally Todd said "Aunt Tru? Are you SURE my Mom should be riding horses? She fell off her exercise bike last week in the den." Tru laughed out loud while Janet snorted and mimed back handing Todd.

"I imagine your Mom will find her balance in a saddle or she'll have a really long walk back to the cabin." Janet smacked Tru on the back of the head and stalked away to the tack room.

By 8am the four horses saddled and the group was riding down the main road away from the cabin. David and Chris were parked in rocking chairs on the porch, feet braced against the porch railing watching the foursome ride off. Cigar smoke eddied over their heads, mixing with the smell of desert sage and fresh coffee. "Try not to be gone all day ladies! You want to get home in time to make dinner for your men." shouted Chris. The hand gesture he received in reply from both women was not polite. "We packed a sack lunch for ourselves. There's a can of Spam for you MEN!" Tru flung back over her shoulder just as Azul picked up a prancing trot. "See? The key to winning any argument is to be the first to leave the scene of the argument." Tru lectured the kids as the cabin disappeared behind a bend in the road.

The temperature rose as they descended the mountain to the flat desert plain on the back half of the Marcus' property. A half mile meant the balmy 80 degrees at the cabin was now 85 degrees and rising on the horse trail. The ground lost it's rocky edge and became more sand and loose dirt while the mesquite trees flourished in clusters with ocotillo stalks alongside. Roadrunners darted from shaded clumps of mesquite to bunches of desert sage scrub brush as the group rode past. Faint javelina tracks could be seen here and there, and those creepy, curved indentations in the sand that meant a snake had been this way earlier.

Todd walked his horse alongside Tru, asking her a million questions about the land and plants. Jeff listened briefly and interrupted. "Why aren"t there any people out here? Where are the houses and stores?"

Janet looked over her shoulder and admonished him mildly, "Actually that's a good question, despite the fact that you interrupted your brother."

Tru leaned back in her saddle, resting the reins on Azul's neck as she spread her arms out to encompass all they could see around them. "Well guys… where do I start? Allright, deep West Texas is part of the Chihuahua Desert stretching from Mexico north to Texas and parts of New Mexico. This area has seen it's share of tragedy, growth and abundance since man had first made an effort to live there. The Spanish and Indians traveled ageless paths and dry creek beds centuries before. Like the one we're riding in now."" Everyone stopped their horses to look at the dirt and the faint lines etched into the boulders on either side of them.

"So this was a river once? Like what… a hundred years ago?" Jeff seemed doubtful.

"More like a million years ago doofus!" Todd was never slow to assign a new nickname to anyone.

Janet just rolled her eyes and waved a hand at Tru, "Continue please."

Tru urged her horse forward and went on, "Pancho Villa fought here, just a few miles up river from us. Settlers have tried to farm all over this area. Many of them died of drought and starvation. Sheep and cattle ranchers found pockets of grass with underground springs to raise livestock on and they did pretty well at first too. But getting the herds to market was a death march. They had to do cattle drives and such over the mountains and across water-less deserts just to get to a market. You know what does live well out here?"

All three of them turned back in their saddles to look at Tru. ""Something besides snakes and birds thrives out here?" It was Janet.

Tru laughed and said, "Herds of wild burros and wild Mexican cattle still survive and with few predators, they live relatively unmolested throughout the region. There are more donkeys out here than people. That's why your Uncle Chris and I love it out here. It's empty. Vast. Quiet. Wild.""

The boys looked at each other and their Mom and Jeff asked, "If we caught a wild donkey out here, could we keep it? We have a huge yard at home with all that grass."

Janet glared at Tru over her sunglasses, "Great. Thank you so much Trudy, now see what you've done?"

The Marcus' little corner of the Christmas Mountains ran down to the Rio Grande and bordered with Mexico at the southern tip of their property line. A series of arroyos sliced through the land like miniature Grand Canyons. At first glance a passerby might mistake the desert as flat. The reality is a broken, uneven and rough country that could be covered in dry, beige sand and give way to a boulder strewn creek bed with a twenty foot drop off. Water and even edible fruit can be found if one knows what to look for and how to find it during the dry season. Flash floods are a common occurrence during the rainy season. Water sluices over the desert sands, runs into the arroyos, bunching up to create walls of water roaring over everything in it's path. The only warning you might get was the sound of the water already rushing toward you.

      Chris had a favorite saying for first time visitors, more a warning really. "West Texas can and will kill you. Even her prettiest flowers have a thorn attached. Pay attention or pay for a funeral." With less than 15 inches of rain in an average year and extremes of temperatures year round, inexperienced hikers can find themselves felled by heat stroke, thirst and just simple disorientation within a very short span of time. Every year there were deaths reported around the area. Remote and wild means no 911 services and the closest hospital was 120 miles away on a good day. Tru and Chris reveled in the freedom of the desert and it's isolation, but they also respected it's magnificent power.

Chapter Three

"Hey boys! Take the next path to the left and follow it along the mountain line." Tru called out to the twins, bored with the adults were now riding ahead. Five minutes later, both boys were hollering "Hurry Mom! Come see!" The women kicked their horses into a canter and slid to a stop when they reached the boys, who had jumped off their horses and were clambering up over boulders and shale to get closer to an exposed patch of cliff. A cave opening was adjacent, dry, dark and shallow. Tru smiled as she got off Azul and started gathering the dropped reins from the now loose black mares.

Janet gamely climbed over the strewn rocks to catch up with Todd and Jeff. All three stood with eyes wide and huge grins staring at ancient Indian paintings on the rock wall. Depictions of what were clearly horses with faint symbols on their hips and sides stretched several yards along the rock face and ended at the cave entrance. Inside the cave were more drawings in a faint ochre color and still clear black charcoal. This wasn't the only wall or cave in the region with pictographs dating hundreds and maybe thousands of years old, but it was the only one of its kind on Chris and Tru's property

Inside the cave were clear oval depressions in the stone floor where humans had sat around a cook fire for generations. It was a good location, providing a clear view of the surrounding plain. There was even a small artesian spring bubbling up twenty yards further down the mountain face. Hidden and small, it was a tiny oasis that supported cotton wood trees and a small patch of thick, year round grass. This gem was where Tru laid out their picnic lunch and produced four towels from the saddle packs. She made a big production of flapping the towels around and still the boys paid her no attention, they were completely enraptured with the drawings. Finally she whistled to the group and asked "Anyone want to swim?" Whoops and hollers erupted and even Janet ran with the kids to the spring pool. "My God Tru! This is amazing. No wonder you guys are out here so often."

They spent the entire afternoon there, listening to the land speak to them and letting the heat loosen their muscles. By the time they finished resaddling the horses and headed back to the cabin, the sun was beginning to settle in the west. Tru led the way with the boys behind her and Janet bringing up the rear in single file. They were taking a different trail for the return ride. Instead of the hour long free for all route of the morning, this was a shortcut through an arroyo pass and over the lower end of the mountain. It required a single file line at the walk only, but took a mere twenty minutes to arrive at the cabin road.

The horses were bedded down in their stalls, groomed and fed. Chris and David had burgers going on the grill and the kids were drawing straws with Janet for the first hot shower. Tru was still in the barn cleaning up the bridles from the day's ride when she heard a noise. Faint over the sound of the generator behind the house. Like rocks clattering or animals moving around out "there". She paused and listened a moment before taking a flashlight with her and inspecting visually.

She did a full perimeter walk of the barn area and the cabin, but did not go down the road. She stopped and listened intently behind the barn one last time, but heard nothing. "Must be pigs again" she thought and made a mental note to tell Chris later. Her flashlight skimmed the ground as she made her way back to the house. The beam glanced off the ground casually. Tru was feeling tired in a good way and seriously wanted a burger right NOW. She wasn't looking for tracks. Had she been, she might have noticed boot prints just at the edge of the light halo surrounding the cabin. Smooth soled with very pointed toe marks. As if someone had stood there on his tip toes, trying to see more without leaving that one spot and certainly not wanting to be seen. Had Tru been searching the ground with her eyes, instead of imagining her husband laying next to her later, she would have noticed a dusting of cigarette ash and two butts stomped into the ground under the living room window. The window with a full view of the pull out sofa bed. The pull out sofa bed that the twins were sharing at night.

Chapter Four

By the third day of the trip, David and Janet were craving some adult time. They took off on the two black mares for the swimming hole. Tru, Chris and the boys took rifles out to the homemade target range on the east side of the property. Over the years, Chris had spent many a happy hour building and using this range. Tru did the basics to keep her shooting skills up to par and now & then allowed herself to be drawn into a target competition with her husband. Never mind that she could out-shoot him all day long with a pistol. Shotguns and rifles were not her thing. Too much noise, too much kick and frankly just too much macho for her tastes. Today, though, was about teaching Todd and Jeff how to handle a simple .22 rifle and basic still targets - old coffee cans full of sand and the like.

They had barely gotten started when a huge clap of thunder rolled over the sky, shaking the windows in the cabin and the vehicles, echoing off the side of the mountain like an explosion. Within seconds heavy, fat rain drops began to land on the parched ground. Chris scooped up boxes of ammo and the rifle while hollering at the boys to get on up the house before they got soaked. Weather in the Big Bend is capricious and chaotic, totally unpredictable. No rain for seven weeks and then a sudden, instant downpour with lightning and thunder. If nature was really out to make a point, the rain would render roads impassable, covered with inches of mud and rocks. The arroyos might flood for miles in either direction. These things could be resolved in hours or several days, no one ever knew for sure. The desert has her own rules and man's desires hold no power.

When the storm announced its presence, the Burgesses took cover in the painted cave. They even managed to squeeze those big mares in with them. Neither Janet or David was sure if the saddles were water proof and they didn't want to risk ruining them. Tru, Chris and the kids spread out in the living room with grilled cheese sandwiches, peanut butter cookies and a DVD of "Shrek". Waiting it out under an overhang at the back edge of the barn was the pointy toed boot owner. He lit a hand rolled cigarette and watched the smoke vanish in the rain almost as soon as it appeared. He had the information he wanted. "Four adults and two boys. Gringos. Facile....easy." Tonight would be spent making some basic preparations and tomorrow or the next day, the opportunity would present itself to him.

Pulling his hat further down on his head, he strode off into the rain and mud. He moved quickly toward the cover of a line of mesquite trees. Pausing once to glance back at the house, he took note that they still only had two vehicles on the property. Leaving distinct pointed toe prints in the mud, the man made his way to the mesa beyond the cabin where his own little mustang cross stood tied, waiting for him. The Marcuses weren't the only ones who appreciated the value of a good horse in this part of the world. Within two minutes he was entirely out of the line of sight of anyone that might have been watching from the porch.

If a person wanted to fly under the radar in this part of the world, cross country trekking on horseback was the most effective mode of travel. Want to avoid the local Texas State Troopers that periodically appeared on the few paved roads? Ducking the Border Patrol agents on the US side of the Rio Grande? That meant meandering the desert passages and burro trails through the mountains. Even the back roads were under surveillance with weight sensors that could distinguish between an animal or a vehicle.

There were any number of places to cross the river directly with a horse or on foot. The majority of the year the Rio Grande rarely had more than a couple of feet of water in it and even went completely dry in some spots during the summer months. Further downstream after the Pecos River and the Rio Grande converged, a crossing required a bridge, boat or actual swimming. The Mexico side was literally another world. Being spotted or stopped on that side of the river was so unlikely, especially a man on horseback, that stealth was not considered necessary by anyone. Even if someone was seen, nobody actually cared until they entered Texas. The cartels and coyotes plied their trades as easily as a pizza delivery driver might in a big city.

Three hours after riding away from the Marcus cabin, the rain was gone and the stranger was back at his campsite on the south side of the Rio Grande. He pulled a stack of flour tortillas out of his saddle bag and coated them with refried beans from a cast iron pot balanced over an actual campfire. Dinner in hand, he began to outline his observations to the four other men sitting with him. They listened intently, nodding their heads and smoking as a plan came together. Meanwhile... the Burgess and Marcus families bade each other goodnight and went to bed.

Chapter Five

Day four arrived to a chorus of moans, groans and general whining from David and Janet both. Both were walking a little bowlegged and slightly hunched over as they limped into the kitchen for coffee. Chris snickered openly, "You guys are a sorry sight indeed. Mule kick you in your sleep?"

"Chris! Hush. You know we don't have mules." For a moment Janet was hopeful her friend was going to be sympathetic. She was wrong. "Besides you know having sex on that hard cave floor has left your back torqued more than once."

"Et tu Tru?" David gasped with one hand dramatically covering his heart as he staggered backward into the kitchen counter.

"Coffee. Must have coffee. Must never ride horse again. Must beat my children for even saying the word horse again." Janet sat gingerly on a tall kitchen stool at the island, her right hand held out for the mug Tru was pushing her way. Chris tapped Janet's shoulder and slid a bottle of ibuprofen into her left hand. Janet took four pills without a word and passed the bottle to David.

"So I'm guessing you guys won"t be taking the boys riding to the Rio Grande today?" Chris asked with a relatively straight face.

"I don't know much this morning, but I do know this: We damn sure won't be having sex on those rocks again." David sniped while twisting his back around and rolling his neck to try and get some of the kinks out. "Where are my kids anyway?"

"The barn. Feeding the

hor....ummm...equines." Tru stepped back as Janet tossed the ibuprofen bottle at her.

After some food, more ibuprofen and

considerably more coffee, the group decided that Tru would take Todd and Jeff on the river ride. David and Chris were going to head off to Big Bend National Park proper and take a look at Santa Elena Canyon. Janet was staying in the cabin to read and apply liberal amounts of Ben-Gay to her lower back.

"Aunt Tru?" Jeff asked while slathering grape jelly on 6 pieces of bread. Todd stood beside him spreading the peanut butter on anther 6 slices.

Tru was pulling water bottles out of the freezer, ""Yes?"

"If we're riding into Mexico today, shouldn't we be making burritos instead of PB&J?"

"Nope. Not riding into Mexico, just down along the river. We are most definitely staying IN Texas this trip. So PB&J and Cheetos ought to suit us fine. Just like the Comanches ate during their raids on Mexican farms."

"Pants on fire! They did not have Cheetos when the Comanches lived here and you know it! They only had Doritos." Todd piped up. Always the smart ass, that one.

"Put those sandwiches in baggies and then come help me pack these saddle rolls." Tru had three packs set up on the dining table and was double checking the first aid kit. All three rolls would receive a small 9-volt flashlight, four bottles of water, a water repellent poncho, extra halter and lead rope, a cigarette lighter and tiny bit of steel wool in a Ziploc bag. She added handi wipes, tissues and some hard candy to the lunch bag. Tru"s saddle roll also held a knife, hoof pick, a collapsible nylon food bowl, and her gun case. That was specially made for her to carry on her saddle or as a fanny pack. The bag was a custom fit for her Glock and two extra magazines. Additionally, it held a small pair of folding binoculars, a whistle and a compass in an exterior pocket. This bag was the one she did not ever leave at home. Chris had put it together for her and when he said it might one day save her life, she didn't doubt him for a second.

"Tru, what's with the duct tape and steel wool?" asked Janet from the sofa. A roll of duct tape was sitting next to the first aid kit on the kitchen island and that is what Janet was pointing at.

"You would be amazed at what you can do with duct tape! Bandage a horse's hoof, fix a broken stirrup, splint a broken arm, patch a hole in a water bottle, you name it and duct tape can do it. The steel wool is a fire starter. You touch a little bit of it to a 9-volt battery and it will spark. If you do that over some dry kindling...voila! Campfire. And it's handy for cleaning stuff." Tru finished closing and tying the saddle rolls. Todd put the sandwiches, chips and three mini bottles of Dr Pepper for Tru in a little zippered insulated bag that would loop over one of the boy's saddle horns for the trip.

Janet was laughing and said "Shit Tru. All you need now is a gingham hoop skirt and a bonnet." She ducked as said roll of tape sailed toward her head.

Passing through the room, Chris caught the tape in both hands and muttered "I don't even want to know" as he tossed it back to Tru. David kissed his wife and snagged the camera bag on his way toward the front door. "Try not have a cat fight while we"re gone or at least not without turning on the video camera first dear.""

The men were pulling down the driveway in Chris' truck as Tru and the kids led the horses out of the barn to the mounting block. At 18 hands high, the black mares were way too tall for either boy to mount without a significant boost of some sort. Azul stood tied nearby, tossing his head with impatience. He was not the sort of horse who appreciated lolly-gagging. Once the boys were mounted and walking some circles, Tru got on Azul and took one last look at everyone's saddle rolls. Making sure things were tied properly and that the sandwich bag was on Jeff's saddle horn. There were no fast food drive through windows where they were going.

Her eyes landed on a zippered rifle case just inside the barn and she paused a moment. Chris always insisted she take the rifle along when she rode to the river. It would stop a criminal, an aggressive javelina or rampaging wild bull, no question about it. But it was also big, required far more effort to use than her handgun and truthfully, she just did not want to get off her horse and go through the rigmarole of attaching it to her saddle. So she left it in the barn and waved for the boys to follow Azul as she rode to the arroyo path, heading south.

Chapter 6 - 12:30pm

Lunch time found the threesome seated under a group of salt cedar trees along the Rio Grande's banks. The kids were scarfing their PB&Js, empty Gatorade bottles at their sides. The horses were grazing with their bridles off. Each had been haltered and tied to a tree so they could have a break too. It was so quiet you could hear the lizards in the grass as they scurried about doing whatever it is that lizards do. The boys had been astonished to see almost no water at all in the riverbed. Despite the previous night's rain, the river was less than a foot deep in some spots and a slow motion trickle was all the movement the water could manage. The light mud showed tracks of javelinas, burros, roadrunners and rabbits all along the ride. It wasn't until they got close to the big river that they began to see signs of large cats and what the boys were convinced was a bear track. Tru was pretty sure it wasn't - the bears tended to stay in the National Park or the mountains on the Mexico side. Three huge vultures floated above them in the clear blue sky. The boys had been shooting pictures with their smartphone cameras all morning. Tru thought "God help Janet if they started emailing all those photos on the drive back to Austin - the data charges will be sky high!"

12:30pm

In the cabin, Janet was asleep in the guestroom. A heavy burrito for lunch practically closed her eyes for her. She slept right through the sounds of two men slashing the Suburban tires. She slept through the sounds of two more men on the wrap around porch, peeking in the windows. They did not enter the house, what they wanted was clearly not there. Her subconscious mind registered the acrid scent of cigarette smoke, but did not wake her. By the time she did open her eyes and head out to the porch with a glass of iced tea, the strangers were long gone. She didn't even glance in the direction of the parked Suburban. She didn't want to think about all the packing, loading and driving that would start in the morning. Not looking at the car meant not having to start that mental "Mom" checklist just yet.

12:30pm

David and Chris stood at the base of the magnificent Santa Elena Canyon, their feet sinking in the sandy beach like river front. Here the Rio Grande became mighty indeed. The waters from two other rivers converged up river several miles and joined the Rio Grande producing gorgeous, deep, fast moving water through the canyon walls and beyond. They had driven to the Chisos Lodge in the Park for lunch and checked out some other sites along the way. Mule Ears and the Window offered spectacular natural rock formations and views for miles. The Canyon was the last stop before the 40 mile drive back to the cabin. Chris kept feeling the hairs on the back of his neck standing up; he did not see any obvious danger, but his gut instinct was that something was not right somewhere in his world.

"David, let's head on to the house. See what's up with the girls." Chris started walking back to the truck. He just couldn't shake the sense that something was coming. Like seeing a black cloud in the distance, knowing a storm was on the way, but not when or how severe.

1:30pm

An hour later they pulled up to the cabin and David stared at his Suburban as they pulled alongside. "What the hell? Chris! Check this out, I've got two flat tires. They weren't flat this morning. Did Janet go somewhere and pick up a nail?" Chris parked and they both got out to take a closer look at the Suburban.

"David, you've got FOUR flat tires here" Chris called out as he walked to the far side of the Suburban. There were no tire marks to indicate the vehicle had been moved, but there were several distinct foot prints in the dirt close to it. A closer look revealed puncture marks in each one. "Run inside and check on Janet. NOW." Chris reached into his pants pocket and pulled out a two shot derringer. He followed the footsteps away from the Suburban to the front porch. His skin crawling with each step, his heart pounding with dread.

There were no signs of breaking and entering and nothing was visibly disturbed beyond the SUV tires. Chris made a beeline to the barn and David burst into the front door hollering his wife's name. Janet poked her head out of the bathroom with a toothbrush in her mouth and a question mark on her face. David stopped short, his relief palpable. "Whas goin' on?" Janet asked around the mouth full of toothpaste.

Chris stepped inside the front door with the only question that mattered, "Where are the kids and Tru?" The barn had held only Whiskey, his bay mare, no sign of the other horses, the twins or Tru. The only other thing that seemed out of ordinary was his Savage Scout 10 carbine rifle still in it's case leaning just inside the barn door. The rifle Tru had decided not to take with her that morning. The sight of it untouched made Chris' blood run cold.

Chapter 7 1:30pm

Tru and the boys finished bridling all three horses in the shade next to the river and discussed which way to go next. Tru handed Jeff her compass and showed him how to navigate using the tallest mountain peak as a point of reference. "See that peak that looks a little like Snoopy on his dog house? You keep that to your left and follow the compass North East. If you do that it will take about a half hour from this spot to reach that giant arroyo where you guys thought you saw bear tracks. Keep on the same heading with Snoopy on your left, the arroyo behind you and you'll get to our painted cave in another half hour or so if you just walk your horses."

"That is so cool! We just use GPS in our cell phones at home, but you can use this stuff anywhere!" Tru smiled and reminded them that as recently as 15 years ago there was no GPS in cell phones. "Can we ride down the river a ways before we head back to the cabin?""

"Works for me. Jeff you can hang on to the compass if you want. I know my way home already." Tru gathered up all their trash, empty bottles and stuffed it all back in the lunch bag. Tru tied it to her saddle horn for the ride home. "Pack out what you bring in guys. We never leave trash of any kind out here." The boys did a final visual sweep and found nothing left behind. The only signs they had even been there were the piles of horse poop near the trees and some flattened grass. Tru led Todd"s mare up to a fallen tree trunk and held her still while he scrambled up into the saddle. The process was repeated for Jeff and then Tru mounted Azul, who tossed his head, arched his neck and offered a jaunty elevated trot as he passed the mares to take the lead. The path along the river was narrow and sometimes led down into the river bed itself. It was a single file line or nothing through the thick under brush and overgrowth.

Tru sat easily in the saddle, Azul had been her partner and her friend for ten years. He was still a little wild in some respects. He would rarely tolerate another person on his back, why he let Tru ride him that first time was a mystery to all, but from that moment forward, she had been his person. If Azul acted like there was danger ahead or refused to take a certain path, Tru listened to him. Trust in her horse had kept them both from falling into unseen holes on the trail and once Azul had even alerted to a mountain lion ahead before Tru had any clue something was out there. Today was no different.

Azul had stopped suddenly, ears moving from side to side and his tail was swishing behind him. A clear sign of agitation. He blew softly through both nostrils and pawed the ground once with a front foot. The mares behind him stood with ears pricked, listening to something moving in the brush just in to the side and slightly behind them on the river bank. The scent of cigarettes wafted toward them and Tru knew it was a person out there in the bush rather than some wild animal. The problem in this part of the country was that a person could prove far more dangerous than a mountain lion or wild hog. She leaned over in the saddle and spoke softly to the boys. ""Turn around and ride back to the clearing where we had lunch." The twins nodded and did what they were told without a word. Both mares were antsy and high stepped back up the riverbed toward the clearing. Tru had opened her gun bag and positioned it to put her Glock within easy reach as she followed the kids. Just in case.

A horse whinnied and Todd screamed at the same time. Tru kicked Azul into a full gallop up the river bank and burst into the clearing pulling her handgun as Azul started skidding to a stop. Her heart raced as she saw two skinny Mexican men with tattoos around their necks standing on either side of Todd's horse's head. One was gripping the bridle with both hands, holding her in place while the second had a hand wrapped around Todd"s ankle and stirrup. Jeff was a few feet behind them, trying to keep his mare from rearing and bolting off with him. "RUN JEFF" Tru hollered as Azul came to a full stop, half rearing in the air just feet from Todd's horse. Both the men turned her way. The one with his hands on Todd's ankle was trying to pull him from the saddle forcibly. Tru did not even hesitate, she just shot at the first man holding the bridle. The shot creased his leg, but went wide. It was enough for him to drop the bridle and grab his outer thigh as he fell to the ground.

The sound of the gunshot spooked Todd's mare and she leapt forward in a burst of panicked speed. Todd was bent over the saddle horn, already holding on for dear life against the man yanking on his legs. He just held on tighter and closed his eyes as the horse burst away from the clearing, heading for the flat ground of the desert and home.

Azul jigged to the side as the gun went off, ears laid flat on his head. He wanted to spin and run, but his training took over and he held. Tru took aim at the second man as Jeff dug his heels into his mare"s sides and shot off after his brother. "One step and I'll Goddamn kill you." Tru snarled, waiting a moment or two for Jeff to gain some distance. The man Tru had shot lurched up on his knees, one hand plastered to his outer thigh, blood running over his fingers and soaking his pants leg. His buddy inched closer to him never breaking Tru's gaze. She lowered her weapon a couple of inches, taking clear aim at his groin area. Not a kill shot, but one that would amuse the hell out of her. She gently rubbed Azul's ribs with her left foot and he sidestepped to the right, bringing her parallel with the two men. "Get on your knees and keep your hands behind your head."" It was all she could do to get the words out instead of just killing them both outright. She knew she had to get moving, find the kids and get them home. But she also had no idea what mode of transportation these two idiots had or if there were more of them out there somewhere. It was a catch-22.

The injured man moaned a little and looked considerably paler by the minute. A green ink tattoo with the name "Miguel" was scrolled over the back of his hand. He was losing a lot of blood, it wasn"t an artery wound or he would have already bled out, but significant none the less. The second man looked up at her and said in broken English, "Senora.... por favor.... he needs a doctor. Assistancia. Please."

"Carry him over the river and go home if you can. Don't ever let me see you on THIS side of the river again."" Tru tightened both legs against Azul's sides and he shot away from the clearing, following the mare's panicked path. She bent over his neck, Glock still in her right hand with a round chambered, left hand gripping the reins and some mane hair as Azul picked up speed. His neck stretched out in front of him and his tail flowed behind like a cape in the wind. For the moment Tru wasn"t concerned about steering or direction, she just wanted to put some distance between her and Them. Azul would track the black mares without any prodding from her. It was a stallion thing. As his hoofs pounded out of the soft river earth and transitioned to the hard pack desert sand, second thoughts crowded Tru"s mind. For a split second she felt awful about shooting the guy without any warning, just reacting on gut instinct. It disturbed her a bit to think she would not have hesitated to take his life if pushed. She did grin thinking about what Chris would say if he heard her say those things out loud. Something along the lines of "Kill them all and let God sort 'em out." He wasn't wrong and Tru knew it.

1:55PM

Todd's mare began to slow at the top of the mesa and he was trying to regain control of her and make his hands stop shaking. He managed to get the horse stopped under the shade of several ancient mesquite trees. Both of them were breathing heavily, Todd was almost panting with adrenaline. His horse dropped her head and began to relax. Todd started looking around for Jeff or Tru. He could hear horses and voices beyond the edge of the mesa behind him. Men's voices. He considered dismounting, but there was no way he could climb back up into the saddle without help or something to stand on first. The voices were clear, but speaking Spanish and they weren't coming closer. The horizon was filled with distant mountain peaks, no buildings or roads to be seen. Not even a power or telephone pole marred the view. He pushed his horse further into the little grouping of trees, ducking his head to avoid getting a thorn in the face. The mare valiantly forged ahead despite being poked and scratched on all sides by the needle like thorns. They stood there, concealed from view and listened.

Todd ran his hand down his horse's sweaty neck repeatedly, soothing them both. He could make out at least three distinct voices and they sounded as if they were below him. Todd leaned over in the saddle and pushed some of the mesquite branches back. He could see the trees were actually lining the edge of a cliff like drop off less than twenty feet from where his horse stood. Down in the arroyo were three men mounted on scruffy looking horses, carefully making their way through the loose rocks and mud. They were arguing about something in Spanish. Todd realized these men were not going to help him when he saw two of them had neck tattoos that matched those of the two men in the clearing. Matched the marks on the man Aunt Tru had shot. He held his breath as it began to sink in that Aunt Tru had SHOT a man to protect him. Where was she?

    A flash of movement further down the mesa caught Todd's eye and he squinted, trying to see what it was. Then he realized it was Jeff on his own black horse moving at high speed off the mesa and toward the arroyo below. Todd wanted to scream at his brother, tell him to turn back, to stop, anything! Nothing came out but a croak and Jeff was too far away to have heard him anyway. Todd watched helplessly as Jeff galloped right up to the men, not realizing the danger. He did not know what to do. He had no weapon and he was alone out here. Todd wished he had that .22 rifle Uncle Chris let them shoot the day before. He wished Aunt Tru would ride up with her handgun. He wished his Dad was there. He wished he could just push the reset button like a video game. All the while, he watched in silence as Jeff was surrounded and forced off his mare by the three men.

1:55PM

    Jeff tried to follow his brother's tracks after he lost actual sight of the terrified mare. She was in an all out full speed gallop before Jeff started after them from the clearing. That big mare could cover some ground and she was not waiting around for anyone to catch her. Jeff followed at a more controlled canter, grateful that he and Todd had spent all summer taking riding lessons. He was a better rider than Todd, everyone said so, but this once Jeff wished Todd was the better rider. He was worried that his twin would get thrown off out here in the middle of nowhere. He raked the ground with his eyes; trying to stay on their trail. He was sure Aunt Tru would be right behind him any second and then everything would be fine. Jeff really wanted to high-five her for actually shooting that sleaze bag - how cool was THAT? The guys at school would be amazed.

    The tracks seemed to just vanish before his eyes. Jeff pulled his horse to a stop and then walked a series of circles trying to find them again. He saw some hoof prints in the hard dirt, faint and smaller than the big feet of the Spanish Norman mares. Maybe Azul's feet? That meant Aunt Tru was already out here looking too. Jeff sighed with relief before he urged his horse into a canter and followed the new tracks away from the crest of the mesa. Toward the arroyo.

2:10 PM

    Tru slowed Azul to a calmer trot and began to watch the hoof print trails in front of her more carefully. She pulled up to a stop and looked closely at one set of Spanish Norman prints heading straight for the top of the mesa in front of her. Clearly Todd. The second set were more muddled and circled a number of times before veering off to the right along with smaller hoof marks. "What the hell?" Tru sat very still and listened. Azul had his ears pricked toward the mesa and blew softly as he waited for her decide which trail to follow.

A flash of light caught her attention and Tru squinted hard looking at the top of the mesa. The flash appeared again and a third time. Tru nudged Azul toward the mesa. That flash was definitely some sort of metal or glass reflecting sunlight. Which meant one or both of the boys trying to get her attention. Or more trouble, but either way Tru had to check it out. She crossed her fingers and said a little prayer that it was the twins signaling and not the spark of sun on a gun barrel aimed at her.

2:10pm

Todd tore his eyes away from the scene in the arroyo. He watched another horse slow and stop right where Jeff had stopped a few minutes earlier. This time it was Aunt Tru on her blue-grey horse. Todd was frantic now. If she followed Jeff she would be attacked too and he could not let that happen. A spark of a memory formed in his mind and Todd urged his mare back out of the tree cover to the top edge of the mesa. He twisted the watch on his wrist and tried to make the sun's reflection bounce off of it. The dial was a small square shape so the light bouncing off it was very small. Almost in tears as he watched Tru begin to take a few steps in the direction of the arroyo, Todd jerked his cell phone out of his pocket and held it at an angle to the direct sunlight. The smooth three inch wide surface glimmered and refracted a bright white rectangle of light toward Tru. It took six tries to get her attention. Time seemed to pass in slow motion as Tru turned Azul's head and began to make her way to the mesa and Todd. Relief washed over him. Aunt Tru would know what to do. Maybe together they could rush the men in the arroyo and help Jeff.

2:10 PM

Janet was not sure what she felt. Panic, fear... and honestly she wondered if the men were just over reacting. Tru and the kids weren't supposed to be back until dinner time. There was no evidence that said for sure they were in any kind of trouble out there. She also knew that Chris wouldn't sit around waiting to see if they came home on time or not. He just wasn't that sort of man. She poured a mug of coffee for David and asked Chris what he needed them to do.

"Janet you get in my truck and head to town. Go to the sheriff's office and let them know what was done to your truck. They need to come out here and check things out. David you stay here in case Tru shows up or the boys. I don't want Janet here alone again. Get a rifle out of the gun case and keep it handy. I am going out to find my wife and your kids." Chris looked grim as he doled out instructions and began sorting out a saddle pack to take with him. He wouldn't say anything to Janet, but he knew whoever had cut David's tires was still out there in the desert, looking for something. Or someone.

David got his wife situated in the truck and on her way before he armed himself. Sitting around the cabin was low on his list of things he felt that he should be doing right now, but he knew Chris was right. Janet needed to be out of the line of possible fire and someone had to be here in case Todd, Jeff or Tru showed up in trouble. When he reentered the cabin, David noticed that Chris had finished his saddle roll and was throwing cheese crackers, beef jerky, chips, M&Ms and Gatorade in a little cooler bag like the one Tru had packed lunch in that morning. Pausing a moment, Chris reached back into the refrigerator and snagged a Dr. Pepper for Tru. He made quick trip to the toilet before gathering his supplies and stomping out to the barn to saddle Whiskey.

"Dammit Tru. JUST once do what I ask and take a distance weapon with you." Chris muttered as he grabbed the Scout rifle and removed it from it's case. He quickly checked the sights, the safety, the scope, the bolt action and the magazine status. One 5 round magazine loaded, an extra in the case and one 10 round extended magazine in the case. Twenty one shots including the chambered round. Everything about the weapon was pristine and ready for action. Except it was sitting here in the damn barn instead of out there where it could help his wife. He slipped the rifle into a scabbard on his saddle. David and Chris shook hands, wished each other luck and Chris rode out at a trot. It was 2:40 in the afternoon and he had roughly five hours of daylight left.

Chapter 8

Tru stopped Azul next to Todd with a puff of dust from his hoofs. She immediately looked for Jeff. Todd was so relieved to have her there, he had a hard time speaking at first. "Je..Je..JEFF is down in the arroyo with those guys and they pulled him off his horse and then I saw you and I wanted to yell and I was afraid and what are we going to do to help him Aunt Tru?" the words fell from him so fast, Tru could barely understand him. Todd was about a minute from a full melt down. She reached over to him and pushed his hand gently until it rested on the saddle horn. Using her calmest voice, she said "Breathe honey, just breathe for a second. We'll figure this out and we'll get Jeff. I want you to dismount now and get two bottles of water out of your saddle pack. Can you do that?"

Todd nodded and slid off his horse. Tru followed suit and pulled the collapsible bowl out of her saddle pack. She accepted the two bottles of water from Todd and poured one into the bowl. Azul drank it when offered and she repeated the process for Todd's mare. Then she handed both sets of reins to the boy, returned the bowl, took her folding binoculars out of her gun case and eased into the mesquite thorns to see what was going on in the arroyo below them.

"Fuck." Tru muttered. As she watched, Jeff was pulled up from his knees on the ground and pushed roughly toward one of the thin little Mexican horses. Rose, Tru's black mare was standing nearby with one of the thugs on her back. This was not good. Not good at all. Tru was doubly pissed off. They had Jeff and that enraged her. But to steal one of her highdollar purebred horses too? Just pouring salt in the wound. Below her, the party took off at a trot with Jeff in the middle as the men formed a triangle around him. One had a lead rope attached to Jeff's horse's head, preventing him from making an escape.

Tru backed out of the trees, put her binoculars away and took a deep breath before

speaking. Todd stared at her; waiting for her to fix things. "Honey," Tru began, "I need you to go back to the cabin and get Uncle Chris. I am going to follow these guys with Jeff. You have to go alone and get Chris. It's not that far, you can make it in about an hour if you alternate walking and cantering."

"Aunt Tru, I'm not sure if I can find the cabin on my own. I don't have the compass, Jeff does. And what if you need help too while I'm gone?"

Tru drew a circle in the sand with the toe of her boot. Kneeling down she drew numbers like a clock inside the circle. "Ok look here. You remember the Snoopy peak over there? If that is at 11 o'clock on the face here and we're standing at noon on the clock, then the cabin is at roughly 2 o'clock from us. Understand? You keep heading toward 2 on the clock and keep Snoopy at 11 on the clock and you'll get home." She looked intently in his eyes, there was no choice here. Todd HAD to go for help and she had to follow Jeff. Once they were in Mexico, losing him forever was a real possibility and Tru could not let that happen.

"2pm. I can do that Tru!" Todd's whole demeanor changed as he realized he absolutely understood the clock metaphor. "I'll get Chris and Dad and the police. But first... can you turn your back so I can pee over there? I won't be able to get off and on again without help."

Tru couldn't help it, she had to laugh, but she did turn her back. She checked Lilly's hooves for stones and made sure the saddle was secure while she waited on Todd. When he was finished, Tru boosted him up into the saddle and patted Lilly's neck as she gave him some final instructions. Todd smiled grimly down at Tru and said "I'm ok now. I can do this." Tru patted his leg and said "The day you become a man is the day you cowboy up and do the hard stuff. I think today is that day Todd. Now get!"

Tru checked her watch as soon as Todd was cantering away. 2:40pm. She had four or five hours of daylight left and she knew Chris would never catch up to her before dark. She could still see the triad below her with Jeff between them, trotting directly to the Rio Grande. There was no way she could take them all without help, not without risking Jeff's life in the cross fire. Well she could leave a clear enough trail for Chris as she followed them. Tru grinned as she pulled an empty Dr Pepper bottle out of her trash bag and stuck it neck first on a branch of the mesquite tree. The plastic bottle was light and held fast. No way could Chris mistake a Dr Pepper bottle as a message for anyone else, but him.

Azul bumped her arm with his head, eager to be on the move. "Yep big boy. Looks like we are going to Mexico after all."" They slowly descended the mesa lip to the arroyo, the rocks and shale clattering beneath Azul's feet. It sounded like an avalanche to Tru's ear, but she knew they were far enough back from the gang that the noise wouldn"t even register. It was an easy track to follow, four walking/trotting horses didn't exactly disappear against the desert. With the temperature hovering around 90 degrees, no one was going to get in too big a hurry. Kill a horse with heat exhaustion out here and you were as good as dead too. Good guy or bad guy, the rules were still the same.

3:20pm

Chris could see a single rider approaching in the heat shimmer. It was a big horse so it had to be one of his Spanish Normans. He kicked Whiskey into a gallop to meet the rider. He was disappointed to see it was just Todd. There was no one else coming behind him. His instincts had been correct - there was a serious problem out there somewhere. Tru would never have sent one of the boys all the way back alone if she had had any other choices.

Whiskey whinnied with pleasure at the sight of Lilly and Lilly's paced quickened. Mares like nothing more than to be with their own herd and family. While the horses nuzzled each other, Chris got the story from Todd. He dropped his head, took in a deep breath and then asked Todd what he had left in his saddle pack. Todd gave Chris his last bottle of water and two protein bars. Chris showed him the trail Whiskey's hooves had left in the sand and sent him on his last mile to the cabin.

"Wait Chris!" Todd stopped and turned in the saddle just as Chris was gathering his reins. "Aunt Tru said to specifically tell you that you were right and she should have brought the rifle."

Chris reached down and patted the scabbard near his left leg before he replied "At least she said it out loud this time! I'll give it to her when I catch up to her. Oh - be sure to tell your Dad everything you told me, then get Lilly into her stall, groom her really well and feed her. Tru would be furious if she found out we didn't take care of her girls. We'll be back with Jeff before you know it." Silently, he thought to himself, "Mexico. Just great." Clucking to Whiskey he headed south at a canter.

3:30pm

Janet sped to town like a fiend. Every second that passed convinced her that something terrible was going on. She slammed on the brakes and jerked to a full stop in the parking lot of the sheriff's office. Parking lot was overly generous, it was more like a dirt lot with room for the two Sheriff's department pick up trucks and one "visitor". Just as she opened the driver's door a tall, lanky Hispanic man stepped out of the building. His uniform was sharply creased, pressed and starched despite the heat. A crisp and very clean summer straw Stetson rested easily on his bald head. The only sign of living in an actual desert was the persistent thin layer of dust on his black cowboy boots. Even the Texas star badge on his shirt was shiny. The glass Coca-Cola bottle in one hand looked cold and inviting as the condensation rolled down it.

"Ma'm." the sheriff said companionably. "Something got you in stir this afternoon?" Then he took a closer look at the big white Ford F250 truck with the royal blue pinstripe on both sides. The blonde woman walking up to him did not belong to that truck. Neither Chris or Tru Marcus were inside of it, just this stranger and that meant trouble. He straightened up and pushed the door open farther, allowing Janet to enter the air conditioned office.

Janet stopped just inside the building and said ""I need the sheriff. Chris Marcus said to tell you that you need to come to the cabin now. Our Suburban was vandalized and my two kids are out with Tru in the middle of God knows where. Chris said he thinks someone is stalking them out there." She waved her hand in the general direction of Mexico and the Rio Grande.

The sheriff watched her closely, she was agitated and worried, but not hysterical. "Ms....?"

"Burgess, I'm Janet Burgess. Will you please come?"

"Ms. Burgess, I'm happy to go out to the Marcus place with you, don't worry. We just need to get a couple of things straight first, ok?" He was calm and that helped Janet catch her breath too. "Why don't you tell me where Chris is right now and where you think Miz Tru was heading with your kids? Now, I know her pretty well and I find it difficult to believe she's lost. Were they hiking or riding? What time did they leave? And what sort of vandalism was done to your vehicle?"

It took fifteen minutes to get all the information out and on paper. Then Sheriff Ramos got in his own truck and followed Janet back to the cabin. He spoke to his only deputy via the truck's radio and brought him up to date on the developing situation. They decided that Hector would make sure the four wheeler was gassed up and that the department's two horses were sound and ready for a possible search and rescue. The sheriff had been at this job for almost thirty years and was less than a year away from retirement. It never failed that at least three times a year they launched a full manhunt for some lost or dehydrated hiker, photographer or cyclist. He was truly surprised to think that this time, they might be out hunting the Marcus woman. She knew this land, knew the dangers and she made sure her animals were in good enough condition to handle the rigors of the trails out here as well. He savored all the information floating around in his head and chewed on an unlit cigar as he drove. Most likely there was something foul out there which meant Chris Marcus was going to be difficult to handle and impossible to control.

4:00pm

Todd rode directly to the front porch of the cabin, bypassing the barn. Lilly was covered in a layer of sweat and dust and her head was hanging a bit as Todd called out for his Dad. David came running out of the front door with the rifle in the crook of his right arm, pointed at the ground. His heart was racing and his mind wrestled over whether to be relieved to see Todd or terrified that Jeff was not with him. "Son! What the hell is going on? Did you pass Chris out there? Where is Jeff? Are you ok?" David was clearly the genetic link to Todd's rapid fire speech patterns when he was upset.

"Come to the barn with me Dad. I need to put Lilly away and get her some water and food. I saw Chris and he said to tell you he's going to bring Jeff and Aunt Tru back as soon as possible. Oh yeah, he said you need to send the Sheriff out behind him." Todd slid out of the saddle and wobbled a bit as his legs made the adjustment back to a solid surface. "I'll tell you everything in the barn."

4:20pm

Janet roared up to the cabin, parking to the left of her still flat Suburban. Without waiting for the sheriff, she shot up the porch steps, shouting for David, Todd, Jeff and Tru. Sheriff Ramos pulled in at slightly more sedate pace and parked on the other side of the Suburban. The sheriff got out and took a long look at the ruined tires, slowly walked around the entire vehicle and then lit his cigar. With a deep exhalation of breath, he began to walk to the porch of the cabin. His stomach ulcer was beginning that familiar bump and grind that meant he would be chewing another half pack of Rolaids before the day was over.

At the front door, he removed his Stetson and stepped inside without knocking. Had Miz Tru been home he would have knocked and politely waited for her to invite him in and offer a glass of sweet iced tea. Miz Tru was NOT home and that meant good manners were second to getting to the bottom of this little nightmare. Once inside, his eyes adjusted to the darker interior after the blazing sun outside and then narrowed. He saw David hugging his wife with a preteen boy between them and a rifle slung over one arm. Ramos cleared his throat and drawled "Son.... you want to put that rifle down while we talk?""

Chapter 10 4:00pm

Tru glanced at the sky and noted the perfect blue, unmarked by a single cloud as far as the eye could see. That was good and bad. No clouds meant no more rain, but it also meant that tonight would be cold out in the open desert. She had only a light jacket in her saddle pack and a single pair of extra socks. Tru seriously hated being cold. She stopped Azul and looked at the Rio Grande directly in front of them. She could hear the three riders and Jeff a few hundred feet to her right and slightly ahead of her as they crossed the river into Mexico.

Tru considered her options while she listened to their horses' hooves splashing through the low water. She could catch up to them easily enough at this juncture, but with the heavy brush, there was no way she could save Jeff and get him home without finding herself trapped. Going to Mexico in pursuit wasn't a great option either. It meant committing who knows how many felonies on THIS side of the border. Crossing into Mexico armed as well? That alone was a long term prison sentence on the Mexico side of the border. Not to mention the confiscation of her horses. The very thought of her beloved equines being taken and sold in Mexico made her heart constrict a bit. She leaned forward over Azul's neck and rubbed his ears while she whispered an apology to him for the risks she was about to take with all their lives.

Tru eased down the bank and walked up river. When she came to the churned sand where the gang had crossed 10 minutes earlier, she paused. Azul stood stock still, listening with Tru, his head and ears turned south. She could hear them still thrashing around in the brush along the river easement. It was about 200 foot deep and ran the length of the Rio Grande on the Mexico side. Thick, heavy, old growth mesquite trees combined with almost every type of thorned or poisonous bush or plant that the Chihuahua

desert had to offer. Existing roads or paths had to be macheted back weekly or they would quite literally vanish. Tru smiled to herself thinking of these idiots hacking a new trail. She would be able to follow easily enough and not have to do any of that nasty work herself.

Before she followed them, Tru wanted to take a quick look at the clearing where she had shot the first guy earlier. She was sure they were all connected, but she wasn't sure if they had joined the three men with Jeff or were still lurking out here watching her. She walked Azul forward in the river bed, trying to moderate his pace to prevent excessive splashing in the water. The river bank steepened on her right, the underbrush thinned considerably and she dismounted. Leaving Azul standing in the water behind her, she inched forward and peeked over the muddy bank at the clearing where she and the kids had eaten lunch. It was empty. A clear blood trail led to the bank a few feet away from her and across the river.

Tru considered the blood for a moment while she decided what her next move should be. It was important to locate these two men. She damn sure did not want them following HER and ambushing her later while she followed Jeff. Yet following Jeff was exactly what she needed to be doing before they disappeared. She sighed, walked back to Azul and dug around in her saddle bag for a piece of colored string. She had two random lengths of orange hay bale twine in a pocket. She used half of one piece to tie three sticks together in an arrow shape which she placed next to the most obvious line of blood. The arrow pointed due South. Next to it, in the dirt, she used her finger to write the words

"C - 2 men south. 1 shot leg. New trail 3 men, Jeff & me. Luv, Tru"

She drew an arrow to indicate the general direction of the newly cut trail. It was the best she could do right now as far as communicating with her husband. She mounted Azul again, turned around went back downstream until she found the Jeff's trail again. It was 4:40pm.

While Tru was turning South onto the freshly cut path over the river, Sheriff Ramos was on his radio at her cabin directing his deputy to call the Border Patrol for a helicopter pass over of the area. He had listened to the entire story from David and Todd, viewed the flat tires on the Suburban and walked through the house and barn. He put the two hand rolled cigarette butts from under the living room window in a Ziploc baggie for future analysis. The Sheriff cursed under his breath when he heard that Chris had taken off on horseback in search of his wife long ago. That meant Chris was out there in the desert, most likely heading into Mexico armed and angry. The Sheriff had no authority on the other side of the river and could not help any of them once they left Texas. Chris on the other hand, wouldn't give a tinker's damn about the so called border or laws. Not that Sheriff Ramos blamed him, if he were honest, he would do exactly the same thing. 'If you can't stop 'em, dig 'em out of the hole' was the only plan he had right now.

Sheriff Ramos asked the Burgess family if they wanted to go back to town and spend the night at the local motel. They declined, preferring to wait at the cabin in case anyone came home. Ramos nodded and climbed back into his truck, reminding them to keep the doors locked, the lights on and a weapon at hand. He would send the deputy out in the morning to check on them. In the meantime, he had some riding to do himself. A cloud of dust billowed in the late afternoon sun as the sheriff sped away.

At 4:00pm Chris stopped at the mesa top where Todd left Tru earlier. He had ridden Whiskey harder than she deserved, trying to make up some time and hoping to catch his wife before nightfall. Whiskey was sweating and blowing a bit, but she was in excellent condition, so he wasn't worried. He dismounted and pulled Tru's Dr Pepper bottle off the mesquite branch with a grin. Spotting Azul's track down the side of the arroyo was easy enough, Tru had not been in a huge hurry, but she hadn't been making any effort at stealth either. Chris figured he was about an hour behind her, maybe an hour and twenty minutes at the most. He let Whiskey rest for five minutes before he hand walked her down to the arroyo floor. There were signs aplenty down here, horse hooves, boot prints and scuffle marks. It all matched what Todd had told him about Jeff being dragged to the ground and three other mounted men. Straight through the middle of all that ruckus were Azul's prints making a four beat trot pattern directly to the mouth of the arroyo and into the desert. Chris got back in the saddle, pulling a packet of cheese crackers out of his bag. One thing was clear, the whole group was heading south toward Mexico. "Well Miss Whisk, it is easier to dump the bodies over there." Chris had a long established habit of talking to his horses and Whiskey tipped an ear in his direction at the sound of his voice. They settled into a relaxed trot for the trek to the river, no sense burning the mare out just yet.

Chapter 11

4:40pm

Jeff was scared, but calm. He knew from Boy Scouts that staying calm in an emergency meant surviving an emergency. What Boy Scouts had not taught him was how to escape a kidnapping. When the fat man had dragged him from Rose's back he had fallen hard on the rocky ground. He was bruised and a little sore, but not injured. Jeff secretly wanted to cry and beg them to leave him alone, but he was twelve now! So in honor of his many years, Jeff instead refused to utter a single sound. The one thought that kept him from crying like a little kid was the memory of a brief glimpse of Aunt Tru as she had started riding down the arroyo lip. He was pretty sure it was Tru anyway and if it was her, then help was coming.

He watched the men on either side of him and glared at the back of the fat one now riding Rose. They all had tattoos encircling their necks, it looked like barbed wire or something similar. All three were Mexican with the deep tans of men who spent all their time out of doors. He knew the fat one was the leader because when he spoke the other two showed deference. The fat one had some sort of an eagle tattoo on his right arm that extended from his elbow down to the wrist. It was a faded greenish color while the barbed wire on his throat was a deep black color.

Jeff wasn't tied up, but even if he yanked his horse's reins and tried to run, the rope attached to her bridle was held by the man on his left. The little palomino gelding he was sitting on had belonged the fat man and Jeff was pretty sure the poor old thing couldn't have run away under any circumstances. He wasn't like Rose who was young and healthy. So Jeff sat silently in the saddle, trying not to panic, trying to make mental notes of anything that seemed important. He clung to the hope that it had been Aunt Tru he saw earlier.

Tru aimed Azul down the freshly hacked path. He quick stepped over the branches on the soft ground and pulled at the bit, wanting to race to reach the horses ahead. Tru held him back to a slow trot or fast walk since she wasn't sure how far ahead the others were. Suddenly the brush broke and the wide plains of the desert opened in front of them. She stopped and sidestepped Azul to the side of the path where a little cover could be found. She could see the four riders clearly as they picked up their pace in on the open ground. They were moving into a canter about two football fields length in front of her. Still heading due South and that gave Tru pause. The only thing ahead of them was a mountain range. No villages, no pueblos, not even a road if she remembered correctly. This was no man's land in the truest sense. There would be scattered subsistence farms on dry, dust laden plots here and there. Free running water would not be found until they were deep into the mountains and food would be scarce for both people and horses. "Ah Hell" Tru's eyes widened as she realized that this no man's land actually WAS one man's land. Carrizo. It was Carrizo's territory.

Jorge Carrizo was the regional drug runner. Carrizo was the local cartel officer and his reputation was known by all on both sides of the border. Ruthless, rumored to be insane, greedy enough to kill entire families and sell the children to the highest bidder. The thing that puzzled Tru was Carrizo's men coming into Texas and snatching a child. She felt certain that this entire situation was not their normal modus operandi. Nonetheless, they HAD done it and now Tru was about to cross more than a national border in pursuit. She was about to ride into a dictatorship.

Tru pulled out her Glock and rechecked the magazine. Five rounds left and one chambered. She had two additional full magazines with six shots each in her gun case. She was going in under armed and alone. "I guess I've done stupider shit, but I can't remember when"" she whispered to Azul. Then she leaned to the right in her saddle and tied the other half of the orange twine to a tree branch. Hopefully Chris would see that and know she had come this way.

Chapter 12

5:00pm

Chris reached the first soft grass indicating the river was close. He stopped Whiskey and let her nibble on the grass while he read the tracks. The four riders had veered to the right and Tru's track had continued on straight to the river bank. Chris was worried about Jeff, but his first priority was his wife. It might not be politically correct or even ethical, but what other people thought had always been low on his priority list. He would find Tru and together they could get Jeff back.

When he reached the clearing and the blood trail, his heart skipped a beat for a moment. Then he realized there were two sets of foot prints that went with the blood drops. Both belonged to men in cowboy boots and not Tru's lace up paddock boots. Good. He dismounted, letting Whiskey stand "ground tied" with the reins trailing the dirt in front of her. The mare shook her whole body and then took a drink while Chris retraced Tru's earlier steps up the bank. He found the message drawn in the soft dirt and the arrow with the orange baling twine. "Well that explains all the traffic" he thought.

Chris mounted Whiskey again and set off with the blood trail. He felt strongly that he could find these two on foot. Even if they had horses waiting on the Mexico side, the leg wound would mean slow going. Chris" plan was simple really. Get close enough to execute both of the men and then get back on Tru's trail. No sense in letting them recover to meet up with the other three holding Jeff. Or worse, end up cold cocking his wife from behind.

As soon as the woods opened up to the desert valley Chris saw the pair. They were about a mile ahead, riding double on one horse with the second horse trailing loose alongside. There was no sign of anyone else as far as the eye could see. Chris paused before riding out into the open. He knew this was Carrizo territory and he prayed that Tru remembered that fact as well. Killing two of Carrizo's men was going to cause a serious ruckus and killing five of them would start a war. That was fine with Chris, it was the how of it all that made him stop and think. Without being aware that he was speaking out loud, Chris muttered "Whiskey…let's go pick a fight."" He dug his heels into the mare's ribs and she burst forward out of the mesquite trees.

5:00pm

Sheriff Ramos traded his pick up truck for a black and white spotted Appaloosa horse. The gelding was technically owned by the county, but had spent all 8 years of his life in Ramos' barn. Tiger was persnickety and prone to spooking at plastic bags, but he was surefooted and had stamina to spare. The sheriff figured they would get out to the river and see what was what, but he knew there would be no catching up to Tru and the boy, not this late in the day and certainly not with a 2 hour head start. As to Chris…well he might find him, but getting him to come back without his wife, that was a fantasy.

The Border Patrol chopper had reported seeing riders just south of the river less than a half hour earlier. They were forbidden from crossing into Mexican airspace, so the visual was made with binoculars while flying parallel to the Rio Grande. No real details, just a rough head count that said four, maybe six people on horseback moving south, away from Texas. They thought they had seen another single rider at the river, but could not confirm. Ramos" home was a mile north of the river, but at best he was two miles upstream from the sightings. He would cut cross country to save some time and distance.

The sheriff's wife brought him two cold pot roast sandwiches, a pair of 2 liter bottles of iced water, and a single bottle of Snapple Ice Tea. He put it all in his saddle bag and kissed her cheek. ""I guess you'll be up at the Marcus place with the rest of that roast while I'm gone?" His wife was always doing that sort of thing, she firmly believed that food could cure everything from a cold to full on heartbreak.

"And what's left of the apple pie. That poor woman must be out of her mind with worry!" She patted his hand and added "Do me a favor? Don't be out all night, you've only got 2 hours of daylight left. If you decide you need to go into Mexico, don't go alone."

Ramos tipped his Stetson to his wife and swung up into the saddle. "Si, Senora." He turned Tiger to the well worn dirt road leading to the river and was gone. Hector, his deputy would already be there waiting.

Chapter 13

5:45pm

    The sheriff and Hector stalked around the clearing, eyeballing the blood pooled on the ground where Tru had shot the man earlier in the afternoon. It was drying and congealed. Vultures had been checking out the area when they had arrived. They followed the blood drops on foot to the center of the river bed and stopped. It was clear what happened. Hector knelt on one knee in front of Tru's message for Chris and said "Boss, do you think Chris Marcus saw this?"

    Ramos had tilted his hat off his forehead and stood with his hands on his hips, staring into Mexico. He glanced Hector's way and nodded. "I can promise you he's been through here long ago. And he went after the crippled one. He'll finish him off and then go get Tru and that boy."

    "That's murder! You don't really think Mr. Marcus is crazy do you?" Hector leapt up to his feet. Young and full of righteous law abiding anger.

    The sheriff gave an exasperated sigh and replied ""Hector when you get married you'll understand. You can talk about law and rules all day long, but in the end, a man takes care of his family any way he can find. Now we have a choice here. We can say we've done our duty, do the legal thing and head back to the office to write all this mess up. Or we can do the right thing."

Hector stared at his boss for a long minute before answering. "I'm going back to the office. You do what you want, I won't get in your way, but I ain't hunting two of Carrizo"s boys in their own backyard."

The sheriff stiffened slightly. No one had said a word about Carrizo, hell he hadn't even thought about that as a possible connection himself. It was promising to be a long, ugly night. "Take the four wheeler down river a bit and make sure we haven't missed anything Hector. I"ll wait here for you."

Hector roared away, kicking up some mud from the wheels. Seeing nothing of importance and not another living soul around, he pulled the county satellite phone from a vest pocket. With his thumb he entered the code for the first speed dial number. Two rings and a voice mail beep sounded seconds later. In a low voice Hector left a terse message "They have the package."" No sense in mentioning Chris or Tru. Hector was convinced that Carrizo"s men or the desert would take care of that little complication. After hanging up, he opened the phone's menu and deleted both the record of the last call and the speed dial code from it's memory. He wasn't worried about Sheriff Ramos questioning the Mexican phone number showing up next week on the bill. It was part of Hector's job to review and pay the monthly office utility bills. Keeping his extra curricular communications secret was ridiculously easy.

Hector drove back to the clearing and saw the sheriff bent over his horse's front foot. "No one else out here Boss. You ready to head back or is Tiger lame?"

"He's fine, just checking for stones." Ramos stood up, rubbing his lower back with one hand. Thirty years on the job out here had done a number on his back, neck and hips. Riding off into the sunset was a younger man's game. "Give me the satellite phone and your spare magazine, then head on back. I'm going to take a look at Mexico. Maybe I can persuade Mr. Marcus to come on back with me."

"Sheriff… that is not a good idea and you know it. First if you get caught it will mean you lose your job and your pension. You could get killed out there with no backup." Hector wanted Ramos to go home. To stay out of this entire situation. Mostly though, Hector just did not want to get involved himself. He revved the engine of the four wheeler impatiently.

"Just do as I ask Hector." Ramos" voice revealed his aggravation. He liked Hector well enough, the man had done a fair job in the last two years, but he never had a passion for the land or the people. Perfunctory was the only description Ramos could come up with. Everything Hector did was basic and just enough to meet the job requirements, never above and beyond. Never a minute of overtime on his weekly time sheets, never a gallon of gasoline unaccounted for in his duty truck even. Ramos doubted if Hector wasted an extra stroke to wipe his ass in the mornings. "I'm not going over the river in an official capacity, just taking a look for a friend who might be lost. Comprehende?"

Hector sighed and tossed the sat phone to his boss and the only extra magazine he had on his person. They both carried the same Colt 1911 pistols and the .45 caliber ammo was swappable. Each mag carried seven bullets. More often than not the only thing either the Sheriff or Hector shot at was javelina or targets at the range. Ramos caught the phone in one hand, put it in his shirt pocket and used both hands to snatch the magazine out of the air. He stuffed it in his pants pocket with the two others he always carried. He wished he had brought a shotgun with him, but 28 rounds in his pistol was what he had and it would have to do.

Hector shook his head and rode the four wheeler back toward home. If Sheriff Ramos wanted in the middle of this goose chase, who was he to stop him? All he wanted was to go back to town and wait on his regular cash delivery in the morning. He told himself it wasn't "blood money", it was a show of appreciation for the information he provided. That"s all. What they did with the info was not his concern.

Chapter 14

6:20pm

    Chris kneeled next to Whiskey, slightly behind a huge agave plant and watched the injured man below him as he sagged against his friend's back on the same horse. Chris was roughly 300 yards away, parked on a ridge, watching them descend slowly in front of him. The agave was enormous, at least 4 foot in diameter and 3 foot tall. Its sharp pointed, arrow shaped leaves offered as much cover as he was going to get out here in the open. Dusk was settling in, but the purple and pink light was still strong enough to reveal Chris clearly if either of the two men had bothered to turn around and look behind them. They did not.

    Chris removed the Savage Scout from its scabbard and ground tied Whiskey a few feet away. She was gun broke and should stay close when the shots were fired. On the off chance that she did panic, Chris wanted her several feet away to reduce the risk of being run over. Currently she was nibbling on what few pieces of scrub grass she could find and paying Chris no attention whatsoever.

    He would have preferred to have a small bipod or a level log of some type to brace the rifle while he lined up his shot. What he found was a smallish boulder and he made the most of it. The scope on the rifle was a four power fixed and would give Chris more than enough visual clarity to take both shots from a prone position, even in the failing light. He breathed slowly and easily, taking his time in lining up the first shot. The riders were still on a single horse and moving at a slow walk in a straight line. Carrying the two of them had evidently worn the little Mexican horse down, he might bolt when the first crack of the rifle sounded, but he wouldn't go far or fast for long. Chris had considered just shooting the horse dead under the two men, but the whole idea struck him as unnecessarily cruel.

Chris squeezed the trigger evenly and watched the head of the first man explode just as the sound of the weapon registered in the horse's ears. He had taken out the uninjured man first as he was the one most likely to be able to run or return fire. Since this wasn't a duel and was in fact an execution, fair play was not on Chris' agenda. He even grinned a little as he watched their horse shy left and begin to spin around, heading back toward Chris' position. The second man was the one with the leg wound from Tru's pistol. He was trying to grab the reins and slide forward in the saddle as his amigo fell to the ground with half his head disintegrated. The swollen leg wasn't cooperating, he kept kicking the horse in the flank. A panicked horse is most likely to bolt and flee at top speed from perceived danger. A panicked horse already fleeing and then feeling a kick or bite on his upper body will add a round of high bucks and twists to his getaway run. Chris knew this and watched patiently as the injured man lost control of his body and flopped to the ground, bouncing off a number of cactus and agave plants before coming to a crumpled, moaning stop.

The horse leaped in fear, changing direction once more and following the second horse that had been traveling alongside them earlier. Chris sat another five minutes, just watching the fallen man through his rifle scope, listening to Whiskey chewing behind him, waiting to see if anyone else would stumble onto the tableau. He briefly considered just leaving the man out there on foot, seriously handicapped and going on about his business of finding his wife and Jeff. However, this was cartel territory and that meant traffic. Or possible help for the fool, which could end up biting Chris in the ass later. Instead of leaving, Chris gathered up Whiskey's reins, mounted and rode down to have a little conversation with the man before he put him out of his misery.

6:30pm

Sheriff Ramos pulled Tiger to a skidding halt when he heard the report of Chris' rifle in the distance. He had been moving at an easy canter toward a ridge in the distance. Ramos knew if he were in Chris' shoes right now, that ridge offered the best high ground to mount an attack. Then the shot rang out, reverberating off the desert floor and forming a spooky sort of echo. Ramos sat still on Tiger, listening and watching. He was out in the open and pretty confident Mr. Marcus would not shoot him, but a little caution still might be called for all the same. After five minutes with no second shot fired, Ramos tugged his Stetson a little tighter on his head and then unsnapped his weapon holster. He nudged Tiger back up to speed and decided to sweep to the left of the ridge and come up on the far side rather than taking it head on.

6:35pm

Chris dismounted and dug out his thin deerskin riding gloves. Pulling the gloves on each hand, he poked the prone man with the toe of his boot in a rib. A groan of pain was the only response. Chris knelt next to the man's head and poked him on the forehead with the Glock barrel this time. "Hey cabrone! Wake up." Chris' tone was nasty, his eyes utterly cold.

"Senor… help me. My horse…..mi compadre est muerto." The wounded man was clearly weak and in agony. He tried to wave a hand in the air, but could only lift three fingers.

"I know he's dead. I killed him. You remember the woman and children in the clearing today? The lady who shot you? Where are they headed?"

"Water, do you have agua?"

"Tell me where your other friends are taking my wife and the boy." Chris narrowed his eyes and tapped at the man"s chest with his gun barrel. "Don't tell me and I'll use three bullets to kill you. One in your good leg, one in your foot and one in the gut. It won't be a clean or fast death. It's even possible the vultures will start on you before you take your last breath."

"I…I…don't know where they are going. Maybe the campesino in the mountain. Or maybe the rancho West of here." He was panting with pain and fear as he rasped the words.

Chris casually shifted the Glock so the barrel was pointing directly at the man's uninjured leg. He softly rubbed the leg and whispered "This looks like a good spot. At this range, the bullet will shatter your tibia on it's way through. Want to add any details to those locations while you still can?"

"The campesino!! They will go to the campesino in the mountain straight ahead. Box canyon, pequito rio, agua dulce y fresco. Full day ride from here." Just as the last word left his lips, his urine let loose and soaked the ground where he lay.

"A canyon with fresh, sweet water. Got it. Do you remember leaping out at my wife and those kids? Do you remember the fear on their faces? Do you remember how you thought they were weak and easy pickings?" Chris gave the man an utterly feral smile and continued in a whisper. "Right now you feel like my wife did. Afraid, pissing yourself even. But the difference now is that I don't feel what you did when you tried to attack her. I feel nothing for you at all." Chris backed up a bit, put the gun to the man's ear and pulled the trigger.

Chris dusted his pants legs off and made sure there wasn't excessive blood spatter on his boots before checking both dead bodies. He pocketed both the men's watches, proof of their passing if he needed it. He ran his hands in and out of all their pockets and removed their boots. The first one down had a cell phone and some US dollars stashed in his left boot. Chris left the cash, but pocketed the phone. It was possible he could reach Carrizo with it if it came to that later.

Sheriff Ramos heard the second shot just as he rounded the ridge on the far side from Chris. He slowed Tiger to a walk and kept going. He knew what had just happened and why. He did not necessarily agree with Chris" method, but he could understand it. Chris had his back turned to him as he rode up. He did not stop shaking the last boot, instead he turned his head and stared at the Sheriff over his shoulder. "Evening Sheriff."

Sheriff Ramos pulled Tiger to a halt and leaned forward in his saddle, arms crossed over the saddle horn. "Evening Mr. Marcus. I reckon you ought to call me Jonathon right about now."

"That right? Are you going to arrest me, but be friendly about it?" Chris stood up slowly "I'm going to holster my weapon, Jonathon. I got no beef with you." Then he turned to face the older man eye to eye.

Sheriff Ramos dismounted and held his hand out to Chris. Chris raised his eyebrows for a second, then shook the older man's hand heartily. Ramos reached to his chest pocket and pulled out two cigars, offered one to Chris, silently lighting his own. As he returned the lighter to his pocket, his hand brushed over the Texas badge pinned to his shirt.

"Is that going to be a problem for you Jonathon?" Chris asked wryly, nodding at the badge.

Chapter 15

6:30pm

Mrs. Ramos knocked on the door of the Marcus cabin, her hands full with a large nylon soft side cooler. "Mrs. Burgess? I"m the sheriff's wife. I brought ya'll some supper." David answered the door cautiously, rifle in one hand and looked her up and down before inviting her inside. He made sure the dead-bolt was turned before calling Janet and Todd out of the bedroom.

Mrs. Ramos opened the cooler and laid out multiple containers on the mesquite wood dining table. They held a pot roast with potatoes and carrots, had home made rolls, fresh salad, and apple pie. The last container was full of what looked like scrambled eggs mixed with cheese and sausage. The homey aroma drew the family around the table in awe. "Mrs. Ramos…You are so kind! You did not have to do all this." Janet impulsively hugged the other woman.

"Oh honey. It's nothing. Really. And call me Anne. Mrs. Ramos is my husband's mother." Anne laughed and bustled around the kitchen gathering plates and silverware. "Besides, I am sure none of you feels like cooking and you think you don't want to eat right now. I promise you that your boy will be back, safe and sound. You need to eat and I needed to cook."

6:40pm

Tru had been following the foursome for two hours, trying her best to keep them in sight ahead of her and not be seen herself. Azul was disgruntled with the slow pace and the scent of one of "his" mares ahead of them. He tossed his head and pranced with impatience. Once Tru thought she had heard gun fire in the distance, even Azul turned his attention west and pricked his ears to listen for a minute, but they heard nothing else. Tru rode along easily, eating half of the last sandwich left from lunch. At one point she had even dismounted and led Azul to give both their backs a break.

She lurked behind small rises or copses of mesquite trees whenever possible to be avoid being spotted. At least once she put a marker out for Chris an empty Cheetos bag tied to an ocotillo arm with another bit of the orange hay string. Once the sun finally set, she would be able to take a more direct approach. For now it was all about the drudgery and boredom. Her focus was drifting to the questions the night ahead offered. Where to sleep? What to eat or drink the next day for her and Azul? Did Chris see her message? Was he in trouble out there? How cold was it really going to be out here in the open? Where the hell were these people going with Jeff? With a sigh, Tru patted Azul's neck and muttered to him "A long, ugly night coming on us, kid."

6:45pm

Jeff was bone tired and he really needed to pee. His vow not to speak to his kidnappers was going to have to be broken or he would humiliate himself. "Ummm… mister? Senor? I need the bathroom." He said it to the man riding on his left, but it was the fat man in front who responded.

"We'll stop soon enough and you can go then." He pressed his spurs into Rose's sides roughly without even glancing back at Jeff. Rose, like all of the Marcus horses, was unused to physical pain or abuse. She half reared and jumped sideways at the unexpected pain. The fat man sat his saddle well and did not fall, but his face was pale and his lips were a thin line. Slapping the side of her neck with the leather reins he snarled "AY! Bitch!" Rose jerked her head, leapt up and forward, trying to escape the devil on her back.

Jeff wanted to laugh out loud, but he held back. Rose was so large and powerful that she could have tossed the man to the ground if she chose. Due to her gentle nature, it would never occur to her to willfully disobey or act violently. So she suffered at the hands of a bully just as Jeff did.

6:45pm

Sheriff Jonathon Ramos took his badge off and held it in his right hand, studying it in silence. In thirty years of service, he had never once removed the badge in the line of duty. Never looked the other way. Long minutes passed and Chris remained silent. Waiting. Jonathon finally heaved a deep sigh and slipped the badge into his shirt pocket with the satellite phone. ""I think it's better if we do things off the record from this point forward. I can't say I think you're doing the right thing here Chris. But to be honest, I'll be damned if I have a better plan.""

Chris nodded and released the breath he hadn't even known he was holding. "We head south to the mountains from here. I want to see if I can reach Tru first though. Cut across the desert moving south east and see if we can cut her off. Then we worry about Jeff."

Ramos wiped his brow with the sleeve of his uniform shirt and turned to mount Tiger again. What was left to say? They both knew the moral costs of committing, witnessing and then ignoring murder were high, but the price of losing Tru and Jeff was incalculable. Chris whistled for Whiskey and she ambled up to him. The sheriff applauded at this. Chris glanced up at him with a grin and said "Coming when called is one of the first things Tru teaches all our horses. She doesn't believe in chasing horses for any reason."" He climbed back in the saddle and the two men walked side by side. "Tru says it's just about respect or some such nonsense. Personally, I"m pretty sure she's just lazy." Chris smiled as a memory came back to him. His wife whistling in a 20 acre field and six horses running to her from all directions. He and the sheriff walked their horses, smoking cigars as the sun dipped behind the mountain range in the distance. Vultures had already begun to settle alongside the two bodies in their wake.

Chapter 16

9:00pm

"FINALLY" Tru muttered. The group had actually stopped. They had paused for ten minutes around 7:30 to use the bathroom and stretch their legs and then right back on the move. She was lurking in the mouth of an arroyo, behind a cluster of blooming yucca plants. The group was about a city block's length in front of her, gathered around a tiny cinder block shack in the middle of nothing and nowhere. There was a small corral with fence posts of ocotillo stalks and some kind of rusty chicken wire. No lights of any kind and it appeared to be deserted. There was no electricity out here or phone. There weren't even any tire marks in the dirt this far into the desert.

Tru dismounted, ground tied Azul and pulled out her folding binoculars. She couldn't see much in the dark, but the moon did give off enough illumination for her to make out basic shapes and movement. She counted the original three bad guys and Jeff. No one new had emerged from the building and Tru was grateful for that.

The fat man pushed Jeff toward the doorway with a rough hand on the back of his neck. The other two men led the horses to the corral and unsaddled them. The fat man came back outside with an armload of hay and tossed it into the pen. The other two pumped some water into two big buckets from a rusted tank behind the house. Then all three went inside and shut the door. The faint light of a single candle shimmered through the only window. Within minutes, the smell of cooking meat and refried beans wafted to Tru on the breeze.

"At least someone out here is getting a hot meal." Tru whispered disgustedly to Azul. She removed his saddle and replaced his bridle with a halter. She let the lead rope drag the ground so Azul could move around to graze on what little vegetation was available. Next she dug into her saddle roll to take stock of her remaining supplies.

Half a peanut butter and jelly sandwich, a single snack size bag of Cheetos, one Dr Pepper, four bottles of water, half a bottle of Gatorade, a handful of hard candy and an unexpected pair of granola bars. Tru eyed them suspiciously. The wrappers were wrinkled and the contents were obviously crushed. She hadn't a clue how long those things had been rattling around in her saddle bag, but she ate both anyway. Next she poured a full bottle of water into the portable bowl for Azul. In the morning she planned to refill the bottle from the tank at the shack and let him drink again there before heading out.

Tru spent another hour watching the square hovel, but there was no more activity outside. She watched Rose nibble at the hay with the other horses in the pen and she appeared sound and uninjured. She ran scenario after scenario through her mind and could not figure a way to get to Jeff on her own. Tru finally pushed the rocks aside under a mesquite tree and behind the yuccas. Then laid down on her back, saddle as a pillow. She had her old riding gloves on to protect her fingers from thorns and the seeping cold. A fire would have been seen immediately from the shack.

10:00pm

Chris and the sheriff had been keeping a steady pace, alternating between a walk and a trot since they left the gully with the two dead men. Twice they had seen hoof prints in the dirt, but only those of a single horse and heading the wrong direction. They were trotting up to some trees with a little grass underneath when Tiger shied sharply away and gave the sheriff a couple of bucks. "Dammit Tiger! Knock it off." Ramos gathered his reins a little shorter, dug his feet into his stirrups and regained control of the twitchy Appaloosa. "Chris - look around for some sort of plastic bag or something on the ground. I have seen this stupid horse stomp a rattle snake to death, but he thinks he's going to be eaten by a damn bag!"

Chris snickered and looked for anything on the ground that would have set Tiger off. Seeing nothing he started looking in the tree branches and then he saw the Cheetos bag tied to one of the trees. "Think I see the problem, Sheriff! Just trash stuck to an ocotillo thorn." Chris rode Whiskey to the bag and took a closer look. "Huh. I think Tru has been through here. Look…. This bag is tied to the branch. With orange hay string." He pointed at it and Ramos approached on foot.

Tiger stood a few feet away, rolling his eyes at the rest of them. "Idiot." Ramos muttered glancing back at his horse as he pulled the Cheetos bag off the tree and put it in his pocket. Chris dismounted and the two men began to search for Tru's track in the sand. They each held small Maglites and panned the ground until they found it. Moving forward 30 feet past the Cheetos tree, Chris spotted the hoof prints of four more horses. What was clearly Azul's track was slightly offset moving in the same direction.

Ramos came up behind Chris, leading both horses and pulled his hat off his head. He scratched at his bald scalp idly as he asked ""So. Now we have proof that she's onto them, but not held by them. Do you want to keep moving or set up camp around here?"

"I need to find them Jonathon. It's that simple. We water the horses and keep moving." Chris pulled a little nylon bowl out his saddle bag, just like the one Tru carried. While Chris poured water and held the bowl for each horse, Ramos pulled out both pot roast sandwiches and offered one to Chris. They spent a half hour resting before striking out once again.

10:00PM

Hector muted the volume on his television and listened closely. He was watching old Friends reruns and waiting for the cash drop. Normally it was done in the morning, but for some reason his contact in Mexico had texted his personal cell phone, saying he would come tonight instead. THUMP. Hector eased to the front door and plastered his eye to the peep hole. There was a duffle bag sitting on the porch and a man pushing a motorcycle down his driveway. The entire situation was odd and sent a prickle of anxiety down Hector's spine. This was NOT the usual pattern.

Normally he would find a manila envelope tucked under a large flower pot on his back porch. The cash inside would be well worn, used bills of varying denominations, but never larger than $20s. The sort of cash any man could be expected to carry in his wallet. The sort of cash it was easy to spend or deposit in a bank account. Hector kept two accounts. The usual checking account at the local bank where his county paycheck was direct deposited and a second, secret account at a large bank in Houston. He made the 1120 mile roundtrip twice a month to make a cash deposit and the payment on a boat he was buying. The boat was in a private marina east of Galveston and would be registered under a false name when he had it paid off. Hector wasn't a man of great vision or imagination, he just wanted a plush berth that would take him around the Caribbean free and clear of all attachments. He wanted enough cash to tell the whole world to kiss his ass and allow him to spend the rest of his days deep sea fishing.

A deputy's salary would never be enough, so he had taken to supplementing his income by providing information to the Carrizo cartel. Small things like a change in Border Patrol schedules, when Sheriff Ramos would be away from the county on business, new types of equipment the county or Border Patrol was testing, and sometimes he would get a specific request from his contact. Like with the Marcus couple and those twins visiting. All they had wanted to know was if the kids and Tru Marcus were heading to the river. Hector called as soon as he saw the three of them cross the last open space just before lunch time. It was no skin off his nose and what those people did with the information was none of his business.

Hector stared at the courier until he started the motorcycle and rode off. Then he eased out of his door and pulled the duffle bag inside. It was heavy. Too heavy. Hector hesitated before pulling the zipper and retrieved a pair of gloves from a kitchen drawer. His gut instinct was not leave any fingerprints on the bag. Inside were several bundles of cash, all wrapped in paper napkins and held together with rubber bands. Some were $50 and $100 denominations. Hector sat on his floor and started counting the cash, this was huge money and his internal greed overrode his sense of self preservation.

Chapter 17

11:00PM

"What in the Hell? Have you LOST your mind?" Tru snarked at Azul as dirt fell on her head and face. She had been lying on her back, with her rain poncho over her body against the chill. Now she was scrambling to her feet, hands brushing sand out of her hair. Azul was happily rolling in the dirt next to her, his feet tossing sand in the air as he scratched his back. "Really? REALLY? You couldn't possibly have done that OVER THERE?" she stamped her foot and waved her poncho in Azul's general direction. He paid her no mind and casually jumped back to his feet, tossing more dust her way as he did a whole body shake.

Since she was up again, Tru pulled out her binoculars and took another look at the shack and corral. No change. The horses were all still there and none of the men or Jeff were outside. She sighed, drank half a bottle of water and laid back down. She still did not know what she was going to do about retrieving Jeff.

11:20 PM

Jeff was wide awake. His body was sore and tired, but his mind was still running at full speed. The men had fed him at least. There was a small wood burning stove in the hovel; with a flat cooking surface on the top. Opening various saddle bags, the men had brought out Tupperware dishes of refried beans, flour tortillas, fresh jalapeños and sliced, cooked goat meat. Everything was tossed into a single cast iron pan on the stove and heated. The fat man had produced a bottle of homemade salsa from his saddle bag and passed it around to everyone. No one really spoke to Jeff, but they did share their food with him as if he were part of the group. Jeff couldn't remember ever being so hungry, the long day riding and adrenaline had made him ravenous. He would have given anything for a big, cold bottle of Dr Pepper to wash down the food, but settled for some warm water.

He had slept for a time after eating, the men laughing and chattering in Spanish around him as they made coffee and added splashes of rum to it. None of them paid him much attention or offered to hurt him. They watched him while managing to essentially ignore his presence at the same time. When he awoke it was late and Jeff had to use the bathroom badly. All the men were asleep on the floor around him except the fat one. He was leaning against the door with his hat pulled over his face. Jeff tip toed to him and reached out to tap him on the shoulder when a fat, dirt caked hand shot out and snatched him by the elbow.

"Go to sleep." The fat man's voice was gruff. He held Jeff's arm lightly, but there no question he could get rough if he chose.

"I need to…do my business! Where is the bathroom?" Jeff was almost crossing his legs with need.

"You can wait for mana. Daylight." Jeff's stomach let out a threatening gurgle and he belched suddenly. ""Ay. Gringos and your weak stomachs." The fat man stood and opened the door a crack to take a look. Seeing nothing out of the ordinary, he stepped aside and motioned for Jeff to go out. "You go right by the building, in that bush. I'll be watching you."

Jeff felt in his pants pocket and found four paper napkins from dinner. It was the closest thing to toilet paper he was going to get tonight. He dashed out to the bush and undid his jeans. The fat man did stay there and watch him dash into the bushes.

Jeff was sure he was going to be up and down all night with his upset stomach. He had inherited David's sensitive intestinal system and it never took much to set either of them off. Todd and Mom could eat a raw frog coated in grease and habernero peppers and not so much as fart. Jeff tried to explain this to the fat man on his third trip outside in forty minutes. The fat man just grunted in disgust and waved him out the door. By the fifth trip, he no longer bothered to stand up or open the door for Jeff.

Midnight

Azul snorted and lifted his head, staring into the night in general direction of the shack. Tru woke up from a light doze and watched him for a minute. Then she pulled out her binoculars to see what he saw. Jeff! Outside, alone between the house and the corral. Azul gave the equine equivalent of a shrug, shook his head and went back to grazing. Tru was frozen with indecision. She wanted to holler and wave to him. She wanted to run down there and snatch him up. She also wanted both of them to get out of this nightmare alive. So she waited and watched as Jeff did his business and then leaned against the side of the building for a moment before going back inside.

"Damn. He has diarrhea. That means dehydration at least." Tru hung her head when she realized what she had seen. She knew without a doubt that she had to get that kid home immediately. He could die very quickly in the desert without adequate, clean water and electrolytes. ""Need a plan. Need a plan." became her mantra as she gathered her things and began to re-saddle Azul.

Midnight

Chris and Ramos were close enough to the cinder block shack to see it's outline in the distance. The moon was not quite full, but with no artificial ambient light, visibility wasn't a problem. They could just make out the basic square shape, but nothing else yet. Both men halted their horses and surveyed the surroundings. The ridge they were sitting on led down to open desert on the right and dropped off into an arroyo directly below them. The arroyo was a dangerous way to go in the darkness, full of boulders and horse tripping loose shale. They didn't notice Tru right away. She was in the shadows; shielded by the mesquites and century plants.

"I vote we split up and come at the house from opposite sides." the sheriff gestured at the building with his hat. Then he pulled his Snapple Tea out and drank half of it.

"Yep." Chris was leaning forward in his saddle, trying to see into the arroyo. "I swear I saw movement down there." Reaching behind him, Chris pulled his rifle out of it's scabbard and sighted the spot with its scope. The four time magnification helped, but it took three long minutes for him to find what he was looking for. ""Son of a bitch." He passed the weapon to Ramos so he could look too. "Down to the mouth, a little to left. I do believe that is my wife.""

"Looks like she's moving out. Horse is saddled and she's moving toward the shack." Ramos lowered the rifle and sighed. "Stick to the plan Chris. You go around wide to the backside of the house. I'll ride down into the arroyo and follow her trail."

They shook hands and separated. Chris kicked Whiskey into a canter, moving along the top of the ridge and praying there were no holes for her to fall into. Sheriff Ramos eased Tiger into the draw and began the steep descent straight down. He had lost sight of Tru and prayed there weren't any booby traps waiting for him.

Midnight

Janet and Anne Ramos sat on the sofa talking quietly. Todd had already been sent to bed and David was snoring soundly in the arm chair. Janet had tried to get Anne to go home earlier, there was no reason for her to stay with them all night. Anne just smiled softly and said "Jonathon won't be home tonight. He will be out there until he gets Jeff back."" Anne was deeply concerned for Janet and the boy's welfare. She and the Sheriff had lost their youngest son just before his 20th birthday in a car wreck. Their surviving son lived in Chicago with a family of his own now. Anne knew about a mother's fear, loss had been a lifelong companion. So she had stayed and Janet found herself deeply comforted by the older woman"s support and comfort.

12:30AM

Jeff walked back outside yet again. All three of the men were asleep inside, snoring and oblivious of his continuing misery. His stomach hurt, his head hurt now as well and he was so tired he could hardly walk the distance required to relieve himself. He was leaning against the corner of the building for a moment when he heard Rose blowing quietly. Not in alarm, more like a greeting to someone she knew. Jeff perked up and inched out to the corral, trying to see what Rose was looking at.

12:30AM

Tru led Azul as close as she dared and ground tied him. His tail swished his displeasure at once again being on the move, but he minded his manners and waited quietly for her to return. Tru crouched down and crab walked to the corral. Rose was standing closest to the gate with her ears up, watching Tru. Tru reached out to touch the mare's nose and keep her from whinnying to Azul. Tru had a loose plan, not a great plan, but better than nothing at all. She wanted to get Rose moved to Azul's hiding place, get her saddled and then go back for Jeff on his next trip outside. Hopefully she could get it all finished in less than fifteen minutes without making any noise.

Jeff watched as Tru appeared at the gate, undoing the latch and placing a halter on Rose's head. She led the mare away into the darkness, closing the corral gate behind her. A stampede would damn sure wake everyone in the neighborhood. Jeff wanted to run along and catch up with Tru, but he did not want to scare her and risk being shot. So he waited.

Tru used Azul's halter to catch Rose. In frustration she realized none of the saddles were outside with the horses. The tack must be in the house with the men and that was a problem. "Just dammit." Tru led Rose up to the ditch she had stashed Azul in and began the process of swapping his saddle onto Rose. Tru could make the trip home bareback, she would be sore and limping for a week afterward, but there was no way Jeff could do it in his condition. Once the horses were ready, Tru edged back into the open and down to the corral. She was prepared to wait for hours, but the moment Jeff stepped outside again, she would be there to get him away.

12:45AM

Chris stopped just before he began the descent off the ridge and took one last look at the square building. He could not see the mouth of the arroyo, but he now had a clear view of the corral and the three horses inside. "Three horses? Where is Rose?" he muttered. He hesitated and sat quietly trying to figure out what was going on down there. He could faintly hear movement of some sort behind the lip of the arroyo, but still couldn"t see anyone due to a ditch full of creosote shrubs. "Tru what are you doing down there?" Chris turned to one side and could just see the sheriff reaching the bottom of the arroyo. He decided to stay put. At least from his vantage point on top of the ridge he would be able to provide some cover fire if all hell broke loose.

1:00AM

Jeff crept to the corral gate and listened for Tru. He had watched her leave with Rose, but another round of stomach cramps forced him to stay put. Now he was upright again and ready to leave no matter what. He and Tru saw each other at the same time and Tru put her finger to her lips to remind Jeff not to make any noise. She waved for him to follow her and they half walked half ran to the ditch. Once there, Tru wrapped her arms around Jeff and kissed the top of his head. She felt like a hundred pounds had been lifted off her shoulders, even for just a moment. She whispered to him to use her cupped hands as a stepping block and get on Rose's back. Once mounted, she wanted him to race through the arroyo and toward Texas as fast as possible. She would be right behind on Azul, but he wasn't to wait for her, just run. Jeff nodded and stifled another belch as he put his left foot into her outstretched hands. Once in the saddle, he squeezed Rose's sides with both calves and kicked her hard with his heels. At the same time Tru slapped her hard on the hindquarters. Rose shot away like an enormous, black cannon ball into the night. Moving directly toward the Sheriff and Tiger.

Tru was just leading Azul to a rock so she could slide up on his bare back when Chris realized Jeff was free and on the move. He whipped Whiskey around and shot back the way he had come on the ridge top.

Chapter 18

1:15am

    Some nights a combination of fate, West Texas bad luck, and worse timing work together and lay even the best plans to waste in one fell swoop. Sheriff Ramos and Jeff saw each other at the same time, both skidding to a halt. The sheriff put Tiger in front of Rose and led the way to the path he had just descended. Jeff followed the uniform with no hesitation. Chris was in a blind spot - not only could he not see into the arroyo, but no one else could see him either. He was moving toward the path that Jeff and Ramos were racing up. Tru had just mounted Azul and was casting one final glance back at the house before following Jeff.

    Fate, bad luck or simply the desert struck two blows simutaneously. A pack of javelina appeared in front of Whiskey on the ridge. They were racing for the arroyo, grunting and slashing the air with sharp, pointed tusks when they crossed Whiskey's line of flight. The front door of the shack burst open and two men ran out waving flashlights and shotguns, yelling in Spanish at full voice. Tru and Azul both lost their focus for just a moment. Tru was using a simple halter with the lead rope tied to either side for her bridle. She had no bit. Azul was tired, worked up by Rose's presence, and he was hungry. Instead of paying attention to Tru, he was concentrating on the scent trail Rose had left in her wake. When the fat man fired a warning shot, shouting for Jeff, Azul was startled and bolted forward five strides. Tru had been looking over her shoulder at the shack just as Azul jumped forward, thrown off balance with no saddle, she fell off. Tru had fallen off horses many times over the years, it was the price of working with young colts. She had only come off of Azul once before, eight years earlier.

The javelina burst out of the brush on all sides of Whiskey and Chris. There had to have been twenty of the pigs and they were in no small rush as they seemed to swarm all around the horse. Whiskey hated pigs and she especially hated them anywhere near her legs. More than once she had trampled a javelina in defense of her own foal. Which is exactly what she started to do now. Rearing, squealing, kicking with her hind feet and snapping with her teeth like a rabid lion. One pig collapsed under her thrashing front hooves and a second one let out a shriek as her hind foot made contact with its shoulder, crippling it. A large boar, hair on its neck bristling and gnashing its fangs lunged at Whiskey's side. Chris just held on for dear life and prayed he and the mare would both survive. While Whiskey and the javelina fought, Jeff and the Sheriff climbed to the ridge and stopped at the opening of the trail. Jeff felt like he was in a monster movie watching wild pigs trying to kill the horse in front of him. The Sheriff took a fast look at the situation, Tiger and Rose were both snorting and stamping their feet. "MOVE NOW BOY!" Ramos slapped Rose with the tips of his leather reins and she galloped on. Ramos took aim at the closest pig with his pistol and fired. Just as his shot made contact with the big boar facing Whiskey down, the shotgun rang out a second time from the shack.

The two men made eye contact and understood instantly what had to happen next. Sheriff Ramos gouged Tiger sharply with his spurs and chased Jeff and Rose. Chris yanked Whiskey's head hard and dug his heels into her ribs forcing her to turn around on the ridgeline. The last of the javelina were speeding down into the arroyo. Chris had a fleeting thought about what in the world might have been chasing them in the first place, but he wasn't really interested. He noticed Whiskey was slowing and her gait felt off, like she was missing a beat every second stride. "SON OF A BITCH!" he shouted and pulled her to a full stop. He could see the shack below and ahead of him. Close enough to be sure two of the men had already finished saddling their horses. He had no idea where the third man or Tru were.

Whiskey was heaving with both ears laid back on her head as he dismounted. One look at her chest explained the problem. Blood ran in rivulets from a gash near her right shoulder. It did not appear to be life threatening, but she damn sure wasn't going anywhere without some first aid. ""Oh baby…I'm sorry." Chris whispered. He was talking to both of his girls as he pulled the medical supplies from his saddle roll.

Chris led Whiskey off the ridge and out of the shack's line of sight before he began to assess her injuries. He shined his Maglite on the wound as he flushed it with a half bottle of water and applied pressure with some of the gauze in the first aid kit. Whiskey was a good sport about everything else in life; her only weakness was wild hogs. She stood still, licking his arms now and then while they waited for the bleeding to abate a little. When it was possible, Chris dropped the gauze on the ground and pulled out a squeeze bottle of wound wash. The mix contained purified water, lidocaine and antiseptic. He liberally doused the area and flashed his light over it again. Whiskey's heart rate had slowed to almost normal again and she was standing with a hind foot cocked in a relaxed manner. The cut wasn't deep enough to require stitches, but it would be sore and tender for days to come.

Chris wasn't sure if it was a javelina tooth or one of their sharp little feet that had hurt her, but there was little he could do about it out here. She would need to rest and there was no way around that fact. Chris laid his forehead against Whiskey's forehead and sighed deeply. He had not seen Tru come up the ridge with Jeff and Ramos. The night air was rent by a haunting shriek. It was Azul screaming from the arroyo floor. For the first time real fear began to knock on the door.

Chapter 19

1:45am

Jeff and Rose ran for what felt like miles. By the time Ramos caught up to them, both horses were lathered with sweat and breathing heavily. The sheriff introduced himself to Jeff and suggested they stop and catch their breath a moment. Back on the ground, Jeff's stomach rumbled and he threw Rose's reins at Ramos so he could bolt behind a bush. When he reemerged, the sheriff handed him three moist wipes in single packets and a pair of Imodium tablets from his own first aid kit. Jeff swallowed the pills with what was left of Aunt Tru's Gatorade. He scrubbed his hands and face with the handi wipes, pulling out a wad of the Mexican napkins to dry the sweat on his brow.

"Can I see those?" Ramos was pointing at the napkins. Jeff shrugged and passed them over. They were plain white paper napkins, but each one had a tiny printed image. An iguana with it's tail in flames, all done in red and green ink. It was distinctive and unforgettable. The flaming iguana was Jorge Carrizo's personal symbol. Everyone in law enforcement on the border knew what it was. "Where did you get these Jeff?" Ramos kept his voice calm, but he was mentally counting the miles back to Texas.

"There was no toilet paper, just these things in that casita or house or whatever it was. I grabbed as many as I could.""

"Gotcha. All right son, we need to get moving. I want us crossing the Rio Grande before sunrise. I want you home with your parents as soon as possible." He stuffed three of the napkins in the plastic bag that held the two cigarette butts from the Marcus cabin.

Ramos boosted Jeff into the saddle and handed him a bottle of Tru's water to drink along the way. Ramos glanced back a few times, but there was no sign of Chris or Tru behind them. He said a little prayer for both of them, crossed himself and set his Stetson straight before he got back on Tiger. He pulled the satellite phone out of his shirt pocket and checked for a signal. One bar and that was sketchy. The next ridge they climbed, he would try to call for backup.

1:55AM

Tru groaned at the pain in her hip, her head, her face and her backside. She had been unconscious, but she had no clue why or for how long. "Why am I upside down?" was the first coherent thought she had. Her next thought was about how sharp the pain in her head was. It seemed to sear through her skull and brain from the back and over her left eye.

She was laying over Azul's back, face forward and he was walking and tossing his head. Every few strides, Azul would stamp a foot which in turn made her head bounce against his ribcage. Each time this sent a sharp throbbing over her entire face, making her want to cry out.

The fat Mexican had found her within seconds of falling off Azul. He fired his shotgun a second time to draw the attention of his partners. Tru's head bounced off a small rock when she landed, but it did not knock her out. What knocked her out was the fat man kicking her in the face. Enraged to see the boy was beyond his grasp, he took it out on Tru as she lay there. His boot made solid contact and her head slammed into the rock again with a faint cracking noise. Tru was out cold, bleeding from a bump on the back of her skull and a cut under her left eye.

    Azul had run a short distance after Tru fell and then stopped. He lunged at the fat man when he kicked Tru, his lips pulled completely back, leaving his teeth exposed. The man kicked Tru a second time, making contact with her hip just as Azul took a hunk of hide out of his forearm with his teeth. Shrieking, the man backed off and took aim at the stallion with his shotgun. It made a hollow clicking noise when he pulled the trigger. He had forgotten to reload in his fury. Azul reared and screamed as he lunged again. The fat man slapped at Azul's head with the shotgun barrel, catching him broadside on the neck. His arm was bleeding freely, the blood disguising the fact that a significant portion of his eagle tattoo was gone. Azul lunged yet again, his front hooves inches from Tru's prone body. This time the shorter of the other two men threw a loop over his head and snatched the rope tight. Azul found himself jerked off balance and he dug his feet into the dirt, throwing his weight against the lasso. Horse and man battled for several long minutes, circling each other. Dust filled the air around them, both were panting for breath and struggling for traction amongst the cactus. As his airway was cutoff by the rope around his throat, Azul stopped moving entirely. He rolled his eyes and bared his teeth, but he did not pull or lunge again.

    All three men watched him warily while they caught their collective breath. The short man bent double with his hands on his knees, the rope loosely resting wrapped around one palm. Blood from multiple rope burn lacerations on his palm and fingers slicked the rope fibers. The third man tossed the saddle Rose had been wearing to the ground alongside Tru and the men had a mini conference, trying to decide how to salvage their entire operation. The short man voted that they shoot both the horse and woman. Walk away from all of it. The other two felt the woman might bring as big a ransom as the kid. If they had known about their two dead compadres, they would have just killed Tru on the spot.

The fat man and the short one held the rope taut while the third man threw the saddle on Azul's back. He had to dodge kicks from the hind feet as he tightened the cinch. His feet took a beating from Azul"s hooves. He was limping and cursing in Spanish when he backed away, but the saddle was on. Azul reared and tried to thrash him with his front feet, but missed as the other two jerked the rope hard, closing off his air again.

The fat man held Azul in place as the other two slung Tru upright between them and walked to the horse. He was perfectly still, nostrils flaring, ears flat on his head, and the whites of his eyes showing as they approached with Tru. He would never strike out with violence at her. They pushed Tru up, laying her on her stomach across the saddle. Azul danced to the side until he felt her begin to slide off and was still once again. The short man slapped blood from his hands onto Tru's jean pockets before he tied her legs to the stirrup. The other one wrapped her hands together with the belt off his pants and removed the fanny pack from her waist. It was her gun bag, with her Glock and ammo neatly packed inside.

The fat one eased up to Azul cautiously, coiling the rope with each step. He slowly reached forward and grabbed the lead rope still hanging off Azul's halter. Azul was quieter now, though still dangerous. The man began to lead him to the corral and Azul went calmly, one ear flicking back and forth toward Tru draped over his back. The lead rope was wrapped around the little palomino gelding's saddle horn as the men mounted for the ride into the mountains.

Chapter 20

2:30am

  Chris missed seeing them leave. He was peeling strips of duct tape and fashioning a pad of gauze to apply to Whiskey's wound. He had found one tiny tube of antibiotic cream in his first aid kit. Using a cotton swab, he carefully coated it on the cut. Whiskey nudged him with her head and he reached into the saddle bag with one hand, the tape and gauze creation in the other. His free hand came out of the bag with a piece of hard peppermint candy. He pulled the plastic wrapper off with his teeth and held the mint out for Whiskey. She delicately lipped it off his palm. She crunched it happily and Chris said "Satisfied now? If you will leave me alone, I can get you bandaged up so we can get out of here."

  Chris eyed the wound and was pleased to see the bleeding had not returned and the antibiotic cream was not oozing or sliding away. He used an alcohol wipe to clean the margins of the wound before packing the gauze on it and duct taping the whole thing in place. Whiskey would loose some hair when it was removed, but it should prevent dirt and sweat from further contaminating the area. When he was done, it looked like a crazy person had been wrapping the poor mare in silver tape. "We need Tru for this stuff Whiskey." Whiskey nudged his arm again and Chris grinned at her.

  Chris led her on foot back to the ridge top and realized that the three Mexican men and their horses were gone. The corral gate was wide open and still no sign of Tru or Azul. He continued walking to the shack, Whiskey was going to need a real drink and whatever hay was left down there before he asked her to resume the pursuit.

2:30AM

Hector was sipping a long neck beer at his ancient, orange formica kitchen table. Lining the entire surface of the table were the stacks of cash. The flaming iguana napkins that had wrapped the stacks earlier were all in his kitchen trash can. All the money was counted, separated by denominations and secured with rubber bands. The total amount was staggering nearly $72,000 dollars. Combined with the $110,000 already sitting in the Houston bank, it would be enough to pay off his boat and live on conservatively for a few years.

Hector was listening to two little voices in his head as he stared at the money. The first voice said to return the duffle bag with every penny. This payoff was too large and clearly not meant for him. The other voice whispered to take it all, get on his boat and get the hell out of Dodge. If he left now, he could be in Houston when the bank opened. If he got a couple hours sleep he could still be there before lunch, before the Sheriff even noticed he was late for work. He drained the beer and almost dropped the bottle when his cell phone rang.

The caller i.d. showed the county satellite phone. Hector sat very still, as if the caller could see through the phone. The cash seeming to glow with each buzz of the phone. Almost as if it was begging to be seen. The noise stopped suddenly and Hector took a deep breath with his eyes closed. Then his land line began to ring. Hector let the machine pick up and heard Sheriff Ramos on the other end. Hector cradled his head in his hands, elbows propped on the table and listened.

"HECTOR! I know it's late. I have the kid and I need back up to meet me at the River in two hours. Repeat - I have the boy. Backup at the river in two hours. Call Border Patrol for a medic as well."

When the line went dead, he dialed into voice mail on his cell phone and heard the same thing again. When he hung up, the voices in his head disconnected as well and he knew his decision was made. It only

took minutes to pack two suitcases with his clothes, a few books and a single framed photo of his grandparents. The duffle bag money went back where it had come from and in the backseat floor board of his personal vehicle. The Ford Escape wasn't fast or flashy and it would not attract unwanted attention. The irony of his situation and the car's name was lost on Hector.

2:30am

The Sheriff and Jeff topped a rise and came to a halt. The horses weren't spent yet, but they were getting close and they were still a long way from home. Ramos knew that resting often and traveling at a steady trot should get everyone home alive and sound. Jeff clambered out of the saddle and made a dash for a patch of creosote bushes once more. His stomach malfunction was easing some. If for no other reason than there was nothing left to get rid of.

While walking around to stretch his cramped back, Ramos pulled out the sat phone, saw he now had two bars of connectivity and promptly dialed Hector's cell phone. He left the voice mail. Then tried the land line. His brow furrowed with irritation when he once again was forced to leave a message. The Deputy knew he was on call if the Sheriff was not in the area. It was the first time Hector had ever failed to answer his cell phone when Ramos called. Jonathon dialed Anne's cell phone number and left her a voice mail as well. He told Anne that he had the boy, he would be back home in the morning, and that he could not reach Hector. He tried one last call, but the connection was gone and the phone just beeped its failed call warning. With a sigh, he told himself he would call the Border Patrol back at the next high spot.

Jeff walked out of the bushes and swigged some water. He stopped after two swallows and held the bottle in front of his face, studying it.

"What's wrong son?"

Jeff turned to the sheriff and shook the bottle. ""If I'm using Aunt Tru's saddle and these supplies are all hers, then that means she's back there with nothing."

Ramos sighed deeply and placed a gentle hand on Jeff's shoulder, he gave the boy a steadying squeeze and said "Miz Tru… she's smart and she'll find your saddle and supplies, you watch and see. Don't forget, Chris is back there with her. The only thing she really needs is for you to get home safe." He handed Jeff Rose's reins and suggested they walk for a bit and give the horses a break. Ramos felt certain a little physical activity would help Jeff clear his head. He kept walking while he popped the last two Rolaids in his pocket.

Chapter 21

10:30PM - Carrizo Compound, Chiuahua City, Mexico

Jorge Carrizo was mad and about to cross to angry as he paced the lush Persian carpet of his bedroom. His wife was crying in an overstuffed arm chair under a tall, mullioned window. He shouted into his cell phone and ran a manicured hand through his salt and pepper hair. The phone had rung an hour earlier with his wife's sister in a state of hysteria. Her son had not returned from the mountain campesino and no one had seen him. Carrizo's nephew by marriage only, but the kid was still family with a direct connection to Jorge. His wife woke him up demanding he find her nephew. Jorge ground his teeth, but began making calls out to the campesino and his personal pilot. His wife could make his life very tedious when she was upset, so he would spend precious time finding the spoiled brat to appease her. But mostly to prevent his sister in law from camping out in his home while they waited for the boy to show up.

"I don't care why he went to the border, I only care about where he is NOW. Miguel is my nephew and he was supposed to be home with his mamma hours ago." His tone was terse as he spoke to his camp boss on the phone. "What do you mean you don't have extra people until daylight? Get out there and find him. Tonight." Carrizo hung up the phone and walked to the teak wood bar in the sitting room of his master suite. He poured his wife a glass of sherry and himself two fingers of fine, aged scotch. As he dropped two squares of ice into his glass, he wondered why the camp boss had been reluctant to send riders out searching for Miguel. There should be at least five men in the camp at any given time, it was the launching point for loading the drug mules before sending them to the United States. The math was quite simple. If Miguel and his friend had gone out alone, there should be five more men to hunt for them.

Carrizo stood at the window with one hand on his wife's shoulder. She was no longer crying, but sipping her sherry and waiting for Jorge to let her know what he planned to do. He might be a wealthy man, a powerful man, a ruthless man who killed with impunity, but he was still a married man. And all married men must make concessions for peace and happiness in their homes. Jorge sighed and swirled the last swallow in his glass before he bent and kissed his wife on the forehead. "Mi amore, I will go myself and supervise the search for Miguel. I think I should pay a visit to the campesino anyway."

He kept his Armani suit, but changed from loafers to crocodile hide boots in a rich burgundy color that matched the crocodile gun holster at the small of his back. Within 10 minutes he was striding from the villa to the hangar at the back of the property. Carrizo owned two small private planes and a four person luxury helicopter. It was his newest toy and an extravagance even for a cartel overlord. He had justified the ridiculous expense because the chopper allowed him faster access to his bases of operation and could be sent into remote locations that lacked the provision for a landing strip. He intended to bring Miguel back to the villa with him and deal with his disrespect privately. Jorge was positive this was something more than a young man failing to keep his word to his mother. The boy had been acting out and overstepping his bounds with Jorge for months.

1:30am

It had taken two hours to reach the mountain camp and another hour to sort out the bullshit from the truth with the camp boss and the girl who cooked for the men based there. Jorge Carrizo had a much clearer picture by the time he sat in the office, eating a plate of chili renenos stuffed with white asadero cheese and a side of refried beans and fresh salsa. He looked at the camp boss over the edge of his plate as he spread beans on a warm tortilla. The man was thin and wiry, with the same barb wire tattoo on his neck that marked membership in Carrizo's organization. He stood on the opposite side of a long mahogany desk from Carrizo with his hands clasped behind his back. The man looked fearful, a light sheen of sweat on his face. Carrizo's personal bodyguard stood to one side of Carrizo, slightly behind his boss, holding a Glock 9mm pistol casually.

"So you are telling me that my only nephew has vanished? Vanished from what should be a secure camp. Vanished and taken four of my men with him while you, the camp boss did nothing? Are you sure this is the story you want me to believe?" Jorge took a bite and chewed, never breaking eye contact with his "boss". "I want to be positive that I understand this situation. It is only when I am uncertain of the facts that people are accidentally…. Well….shall we say, people are injured. Or killed." He dabbed politely at his mouth with a flaming iguana napkin.

"Ahem, Don Carrizo, I knew Miguel wanted to ride to Texas for beer and women. He took Paolo with him. It wasn't until they had been gone several hours that I realized the other three men were gone as well."

Jorge nodded his head sympathetically and said softly, "It is a shame there is no one here in the camp to manage behavior and business." He stared hard at the man before putting a single finger on the body guard's elbow. "Take this outside and send the cook in."

The bodyguard stalked to the camp boss, snatched him by the arm and pushed him out the door. The cook was in the kitchen as they passed through and she immediately darted to the office door. Just as she shut the door behind her, they heard the shots. "Good. One problem corrected. Senora do you have a cake or perhaps some cookies prepared?" She nodded, keeping her shaking hands hidden in the folds of her skirt as she fled back to her kitchen. The only other man in the camp was being escorted by the bodyguard for his own interview with el jefe.

3:00AM

Tru had to get some attention, so she yelled out. The effort left her grinding her teeth and seeing spots from the pain shooting around her skull. The fat man stopped the group and stared at her, Tru was doing her best not to vomit as she lay upside down on Azul's back. He grunted and motioned to the other two men to get her down.

Back on her feet, Tru did vomit. She couldn't help it, being upside down was always a problem for her, even on roller coasters. The fat man handed her a bottle of water and two of the iguana napkins when she was finished. In his broken English, the fat man was matter of fact, "It does not interest me if you live or die. Miguel? He will want to talk to you about the boy. Maybe he thinks you have value, maybe not." Now he pointed to

Azul, "Loco. You ride in the saddle now, but try to run and I will kill the horse." Tru narrowed her eyes and suddenly understood why he had a bloody bandage wrapped around his fore arm. Azul had attacked him. She nodded in understanding and the shorter man cut the binds off her ankles and hands. She was in such poor condition, she couldn't have caused any trouble and they all knew it. "How long before we get where ever you're going?" It felt like she was shouting again, but her voice was barely above a whisper.

The short man was amiable enough and said "Not long Senora, just another half hour or so. Miguel was going to meet us at the casita, but we'll see him at the campesino." He ducked and stopped talking suddenly. The fat man had slapped him on the back of the head without a word, just a glare. The message was clear…shut the hell up.

3:00AM

Chris checked the shack and immediate vicinity carefully before settling inside. He drew a bucket of water from the tank and actually led Whiskey into the little house with him. No sense in leaving her out in the corral where prying eyes would see her. The hay was inside anyway and he did not feel like dragging it out to her. There was also the fact that a horse in the room would alert him to anyone else wandering up. He checked the mare's wound again, got her settled munching hay and laid down on the far side of the room. He planned on a half hour nap before picking up the chase again.

3:30am

Jose rode into the campesino alone, the same way he had left four hours earlier. After Carrizo spoke to the camp boss on the phone, Jose had been sent out on a motorcycle to find Miguel. Jose had found Miguel and his own bodyguard, both dead with their boots off and watches gone. Strangely their cash and wallets were still present. No sign of their horses. Jose had gathered both pairs of boots and wallets to take to Carrizo. The sharply pointed toes on Miguel's boots were unmistakable.

Jose had gone directly to the office with the evidence and the bodyguard escorted him inside. Carrizo studied the wallets for a long time, his face emotionless. "There was no cell phone with the bodies?""

"No."

Carrizo drummed Miguel's wallet on the desk idly. Thinking. Putting some pieces together in his head. Miguel had been whining for months about wanting more responsibility and more money. He wanted his own territory to run, the chance to become like Jorge. Miguel was too young for a move up the ranks, but more importantly, he was impulsive and could not think ahead. This business was like a chess game; every move preplanned and every outcome considered prior to making a move at all. A man who could not control himself, could not lead. No, Carrizo had long ago decided his only child would be groomed for the business - when she graduated from Oxford, of course.

"Did Miguel make contact with anyone on the North side of the rio?" Carrizo was still tapping the wallet on the desk.

"He called the deputy and arranged to pick up the package." Jose was nervous, but not afraid. It struck Carrizo that the difference between this man and the dead camp boss was simple honesty when asked direct questions.

"What package Jose?" Carrizo"s voice was calm, relaxed even. But a tiny twitch under his right eyelid denoted his tension level was rising.

"He took the bag of US Dollars and the men to pick up your package, the boy." Jose was confused, but told what he knew.

"I see. Let me ask you….why would I pay money for a child? Did that strike any one as odd?" Carrizo"s eye tic was speeding up and he had stopped playing with the wallet. ""Jose. Where. Is. My. Money?"

"Miguel took it to pay for the boy Senor."" Jose licked his lips nervously as Carrizo pondered this.

"Indeed. Jose, there was $71,838 US Dollars in the bag. It is the money to pay for transportation of my inventory. Since all of my inventory is still here, you can understand my concern. You stand here and wish me to believe that my nephew, my ONLY MALE relative stole that money and has since been killed out in the desert by persons unknown?" Carrizo did not raise his voice. Instead he stood, shot his wrists through his cuffs, and told the bodyguard to fix him a drink. When he looked at Jose again, he waved a hand dismissively and said "You may go. We will discuss your future in my company tomorrow."

Jose nodded and scurried out the door, his pulse racing and sweat soaking the underarms of his shirt. He paused in the kitchen to catch his breath and then went out to refuel the motorcycle.

Chapter 22

4:20am

Sheriff Ramos stood on a boulder at the top of a tall hillock and dialed Anne. He did not call Border Patrol as he had originally intended. He wanted to give Tru and Chris a fighting chance at getting back first. He was astonished when Anne answered on the third ring. She had left the cabin in order to be at the auto repair shop when it opened promptly at 5am. Anne wanted the owner to retrieve the Burgess's Suburban with his flat bed tow truck. Ramos was thrilled to hear her voice again. He told his wife he anticipated being at their house within 90 minutes. Then almost as an afterthought, he asked her about something that had been niggling in the back of his mind since he first saw Chris with the two dead men. "Honey, do we have any paper napkins at home or in my office that have a drawing of an iguana with a flaming tail?"

"What? No. Why?"

"I'm not actually sure why. It just seems like something I've seen before and can't remember where." Ramos asked her to think about it and meet him at home so they could deliver Jeff to his parents.

"Wait Jonathon! I HAVE seen those iguana things. Hector had them in his desk drawer one day. Remember? When I spilled that entire thermos of coffee at the office, he handed me a wad of napkins and paper towels to wipe it up. It was in March or so I think." The Sheriff grimaced and thanked her before they hung up. He remembered seeing one in the trash that day and wondering which of his prisoners had brought it in with him. Now his gut was telling him it hadn't belonged to a prisoner.

Ramos slipped the phone back in his pocket and helped boost Jeff back into the saddle. The horses were still worn out, but they had benefited from the slower pace. They were close enough to the border to cover the remaining distance much more quickly. The Sheriff needed a change of clothes, a real toilet and a conversation with his deputy.

4:20AM

Chris was groggy as he cleaned Whiskey's wound again and then saddled her. He had applied more antibiotic cream and a layer of paste made from the creosote bushes around the shack. The creosote leaves were mashed with a tiny bit of water and made into a pulpy paste. Supposedly it had some antiinflammatory and analgesic properties. Chris figured it couldn't hurt to try it. At best Whiskey would benefit and at worst, he had wasted a few minutes of his time. Chris yawned loudly and stretched to touch his toes before opening the front door and leading Whiskey back outside. He needed more than a thirty minute nap and so did his horse. She was still as cheerful as ever, but she was obviously less perky than normal.

Whiskey walked easily alongside Chris for a few hundred yards once he found Tru's trail. He watched the mare carefully and saw no signs of a limp or stiffness. So he got back up in the saddle and walked on. His thoughts drifted to Jeff and Sheriff Ramos, wondering if they had made it back to the Rio Grande yet.

4:45am

The fat man pulled his horse to a stop next to a corral made of modern steel panels. The other two men stopped in line behind him. He looked back at Tru and told her to ride into the corral and get off when the gate had been closed and locked. Tru made no reply, simply did as she was told. She would rather have Azul contained safely and not causing trouble than risk these idiots shooting him out of spite. When her feet hit the ground, Tru stumbled as her knees gave out and dizziness washed over her. Evidently she had some sort of concussion was the only thing she could think. She bit back nausea as she unsaddled her stallion yet again. She couldn't lift it, instead just letting the entire saddle slide to the dirt and leaving it where it fell. Tru leaned against Azul's hip to catch her breath. Azul turned his head back to look at her, but he did not so much as shift a foot until she stood upright again.

"Let's go! Vamanos!" it was the fat man holding the gate open slightly for her. His body odor made her gag as she passed him.

"Get my horse some water asshole and for God's sake, find some deodorant!" She held her head high, trying desperately not to throw up in front of these people again. The short man stifled a laugh and pointed Tru toward a mud hut across the compound. She wanted to take note of her surroundings, but her head hurt too badly to concentrate. For a moment she wasn't sure what she was looking at. The campesino she thought they were going to was actually a full blown permanent mountain camp. A typical campesino was normally a temporary location that could be broken down and reconstructed elsewhere as needed. This place was different. Permanent buildings with metal roofs, electricity and plumbing for starters. For crying out loud there was an actual helicopter parked in the center of camp. Realization dawned on her that she was walking through one of Carrizo's bases. Not his home, the electricity clearly came from diesel generators rumbling in the distance. Tru kept her mouth shut and followed the short man into a hut with a dirt floor and a hammock and small card table with two big bottles of water, a trial size bottle of liquid soap, two grimy hand towels and a simple metal bowl.

He stood at the doorway while she washed up and then motioned for her to use the hammock. Tru took one look at the hammock swaying slightly and immediately felt queasy again. "Maybe some food later Senora. But now, you stay here." He produced a roll of duct tape from her own damn saddle bag. Tru wanted to fight, wanted to voice disagreement, but she just couldn't. The pain in her head was holding on just as tight as ever and she was having a hard time keeping her eyes focused.

"Can you at least get me some aspirin and water?" was all she could manage to say and then she sat on the dirt floor with her feet in front of her. The short man handed her a water bottle from the table and a tiny bottle of Excedrin from his vest pocket. Tru swallowed the pills and then he taped her ankles together and started on her hands behind her back.

"Senora Marcus, I am…how you say? Sorry for things." He whispered this to her as he wrapped the tape around her ankles.

Tru stared at him again and whispered back "How do you know me?"

"Aye, Senora. Two years ago, you helped my sister in town. Everyone knows you and these horses on the frontier." He paused and touched her wedding rings, then removed her emerald engagement ring and held it in front of her face. "The others don't see this yet. They see it and they take it." Tru's eyes widened. Losing her engagement ring had never occurred to her. She nodded at the water again and swallowed her ring with some effort. He was gentle with her hands, but did not leave any room for an escape later

Tru coughed as it went down, swigged back more water and asked him his name. "Tonio. I will find food and give your horse water." Then he was gone and Tru was left in silence trying to remember the encounter with his sister. The woman had come over the border from one of the little pueblos with a sick horse. An infection from a mesquite thorn in its hoof or something. Tru had drained the swollen wound site and given the horse an antibiotic injection. She hadn't charged the woman, taking care of sick animals was just what Tru did. Everyone in the area on both sides of the border knew Tru Marcus was a pretty decent field veterinarian. Goats, donkeys, even an old milk cow had appeared in her barn with a variety of ailments and pleas for help. Tru had never turned anyone away despite Chris grousing about the expense of having to bring an entire pharmacy to the cabin every time they visited. Their horses were known by everyone in the area due to their beauty and size. In a region where almost all the local horses were of the quarter horse type with plain looks and less style, the giant Spanish Normans and Andalusian crosses that the Marcus' rode stood out. They were graceful, elegant and flashy.

Tru leaned against the wall and nodded off. The Excedrin had helped her headache and her caffeine craving. Sleeping with a concussion was a bad idea, but there was no way around it. Her last conscious thought was of Chris and hoping he was nearby.

Chapter 23

6:30am

Chris sat in the shade on the upper lip of a box canyon. Whiskey grazed behind him while he surveyed the area through his rifle scope. The canyon was narrow at the opening and widened to a dead end at the back. There was a defined road made of pea gravel leading out and to the south west. At the back of the canyon, against a sheer rock wall, was a small community of buildings, sheds and corrals. Interestingly enough, there was a high end helicopter in the dead center of the camp. The early morning sunshine glinted off it's green paint.

Chris leaned back against a mesquite tree and ate some chips. He washed them down with his last bottle of Gatorade. The camp was actually quite a lot bigger than he had anticipated. With his binoculars, he could make out enough details to start thinking of a plan. There was a small herd of goats in a pen, a couple of cattle in another pen and roughly seven horses in yet a third corral. One of buildings appeared to be a cook house, there was smoke flowing from a chimney and a young woman in an apron carrying a basket of vegetables inside the door. Chris would have given $100 for a plate of hot eggs, bacon and coffee right now. He paused and zoomed in a little on a pen set apart from the rest. There was Azul, eating a pile of hay and what looked like one of Chris' saddles laying in the dirt a few feet away. He was still wearing a halter with a filthy lead rope dangling from it and Chris could clearly see sweat stains on his back.

Chris sat and digested what he was seeing. If Azul was there, Tru was down there. She had to have been under duress or injured to leave her horse and equipment in that state of disarray. There were a number of single room shacks or casitas scattered along the outskirts of the main camp. Barracks or living quarters for the men stationed here? Chris' second question was where were all those men? It was obvious that the camp had a minimum staff on hand. He sighed, put his binoculars back in the saddle bag and proceeded to lead Whiskey down off the top of the ledge. Time to find a place to lay low out of sight and do some more detailed surveillance.

6:30AM

Sheriff Ramos could see his house ahead of them now. The horses were walking steadily, but their heads were drooping and they were no longer pricking their ears or paying attention to low flying birds or lizards in front of their feet. Jeff wasn't much better actually. The boy was going to need rest and he might get away without a trip to the Emergency Room, but he definitely needed some fluids and electrolytes. A bowl of chicken soup would help too.

Anne was pacing on the back porch watching their dust trail inch closer and closer. She had met the service station owner and sent him with the tow truck and a note out to the Marcus cabin, then raced back to her own home. In the hour and a half since she had spoken to Jonathon, she had cleaned out two stalls in their tiny barn, laid new bedding, filled feed and water buckets, and lugged a half bale of hay to each stall. The horses would be fine, it was the child that had Anne chewing her fingernails to nubs.

6:30AM

Todd was the only one awake when the tow truck pulled up behind his parent's Suburban. He went out the front door with the .22 rifle in his hands to see what was up. The driver stepped down and waved at Todd cautiously. "Hey now…don't get excited! My name is Roberto and Miz Anne sent me out to fix your Dad's truck. She also sent a note for you folks. I'll just set it here on the hood of your car and wait in my truck for your parents. OK?"

"OK." was all Todd said and backed into the house, never letting the man leave his eyes. Once he had the front door shut again, he went to shake David awake.

Five minutes later, all three of the Burgesses were huddled around Anne's note and the truck driver was still sitting in his cab.

"Janet - I am in town arranging a tow truck for your Suburban. My husband called and said he does have Jeff and he's OK. They are coming on horseback to my house first and I will drive Jeff back to you as soon as they get here. No word on Chris or Tru yet, but Jeff is FINE. All my love, Anne Ramos"

Todd whooped out loud and hugged his Mom, she just sagged a bit against him with relief. David couldn't stop grinning and was reading the letter out loud a second time. The tow driver decided it was probably safe to exit his truck and came forward to assess the damage to the Suburban.

"Ok Mr. Burgess, I think I can change the rear tires here, but I only have two tires your size with me. We still need to tow it to town." Roberto shrugged apologetically.

"I'll help you change the two. I"m going to send my wife back with you to drive it home and pay you."

"Don't worry about it. Miz Anne put it on the county's tab, said the Sheriff would sign off on it. I don"t know what that's about, but it'll all work out." Roberto smiled, tugged his Houston Astros ball cap a little further over his ears and started gathering his tools together.

6:30AM

Hector was making good time. In two hours he had already reached the intersection with Interstate 10. The six lane interstate ran East and West, cutting across Texas in an 75mph swath. The highway was normally a three hour trek due North from his home, but he knew the State Trooper schedule and there were no speed traps set in the area this week. Hector took advantage of this to cut an hour off his travel time immediately. If he could minimize the need to stop for gas and toilet breaks, he would be in Houston by 11am. A stop at the bank for traveler's checks in his other name and then on to the marina. Barring any complications, he could meet the seller, pay off his boat and be out on the ocean no later than four in the afternoon. The weather forecast was clear and storm free for the Gulf of Mexico and the Yucatan peninsula for the next five days. The only tropical wave out there was on the east coast of Florida. Hector laughed and said out loud "Smoooooooth sailin' ahead." He cranked up some old 80's hair rock, merged into east bound traffic on the interstate and set his cruise control to 78mph.

Chapter 24

7:00am

    Anne Ramos gathered Jeff in her arms and ushered him to inside the house. The Sheriff led both horses to the barn for their own TLC. Jeff was so tired he could barely understand what the nice woman was saying to him. He was gently pushed into a soft, thick sofa with a glass of orange juice. He savored the cool fresh taste and how smooth it was when he swallowed it. The pleasant smell of fresh waffles wafted in from the kitchen while Jeff slouched into the sofa and fell asleep.

    Jonathon Ramos walked in and kissed his wife before doing anything else. She was the kind of woman who defined "keep the home fires burning" and he never forgot how lucky he was to have her. He knew she had a million questions for him, but all she said was "Take those filthy clothes off and get in the shower. Waffles will be ready in ten minutes."" She handed him a cup of coffee loaded with cream and sugar before going on about her business.

    The Sheriff put on another sharply creased, dry cleaned uniform when he stepped out of the shower. He was physically exhausted, but his mind was running on overdrive. He was wracking his brain for every memory concerning Hector and a possible connection with the Carrizo cartel. Something caught and he tiptoed past the sleeping boy on the sofa. In the kitchen he motioned for Anne to follow him outside. "Honey, do you remember over spring break when you and my sister were down in

Galveston? Didn't you tell me you thought saw Hector on a sail boat down there?"

Anne wiped her hands on her apron and thought about what she had seen. "Yes. I could have sworn it was Hector. I never spoke to him or saw him again. Just that one time when Lee and I were doing the deep sea fishing trip. He was with an older white man on a really pretty sail boat. Lee said it looked like the kind of boat in that old movie "Dead Calm"", the kind of boat people use to sail around the world. We had some good jokes about pirates after that."

She chewed a fingernail before adding "But then you said he was at work the next morning. It made no sense. Remember? We laughed and decided that everyone has a secret twin in the world."

"I think something else is going on here. What if it was Hector? Why would he go to Houston on Saturday and drive all the way back on Sunday night?" Ramos sipped his coffee and decided he would go directly to Hector's house instead of his office. First though, some breakfast and a bath for Jeff. That boy smelled like skunk wrapped in horse shit.

They woke Jeff and Anne handed him a thick robe and insisted he change and give her his clothes to wash. Then she sat him at the table for waffles. No bacon since Anne did not want the grease to upset Jeff's stomach again. When he had finished breakfast, Jeff took a shower and laid down on the guest bed, still wearing the robe while his jeans and shirt finished drying. The Sheriff got in his county truck and headed for Hector's house, leaving it to Anne to get the boy cleaned, fed, and reunited with his family.

Sheriff Ramos noted that Hector's personal vehicle was not at the house. There was a single motorcycle track in the driveway and the second county truck was parked under the carport. Ramos looked in the truck and saw nothing amiss. He knocked on the front door and heard nothing inside or out. He tried the door and found it locked. The backdoor was locked, but as with all sliding glass doors, it was easily jimmied. The Sheriff stood quietly in the kitchen after he stepped through the glass door. He heard the air conditioning system kicking on and a faint drip from the only bathroom. No radio, no television, no people. He opened the refrigerator, saw three beer bottles, some milk, cold cuts, a loaf of wheat bread and half chocolate bar wrapped in a paper napkin. Knowing what he would see, Ramos turned the chocolate over and there it was. A bright green iguana with red tail flames. He replaced it carefully where he had found it and sat at the orange kitchen table in the same chair Hector had used hours earlier.

Ramos allowed his eyes to slowly circle the kitchen and living room beyond. Next he stood and went through the medicine cabinet in the bathroom and both bedrooms. All of Hector's uniforms were still in the closet, but it appeared most of his civilian clothes were gone. As was his service pistol and an antique shotgun that Hector had said belonged to his great grandfather. "Where did you go?" the Sheriff muttered as he searched the dresser drawers and bathroom garbage. He went back to the kitchen and poured the contents of the trash can on the table. The napkins that had wrapped the cash bundles spilled out first, then odds and ends from any person's regular day - empty beer bottle, Styrofoam dish from the local Mexican restaurant, plastic utensils, an empty toothpaste box, and half of a deposit receipt stuck to a dried wad of chewing gum.

The receipt showed part of the account number, an amount of $2300.00 and a portion of the bank name, On International Bank. Ramos assumed the "On" was the tail end of "Houston". He pocketed the receipt and a few of the iguana napkins before heading to his office.

8:30AM - Carrizo Camp

Jorge Carrizo stood up from the sofa he had been napping on in the office. He strode to the closet, removed a clean powder blue dress shirt and dove gray suit coat. A short trip to the bathroom and he was freshly shaven, washed and clothed. His temper, however had not improved from the pre-dawn hours. "VIGGO!" Carrizo shouted for his bodyguard.

A simple knock at the door, followed by the man himself within seconds of being summoned. The man looked like a gorilla, as a bodyguard should, but Viggo was more than simple security. He spoke Russian, English, Spanish, and passable German. He looked European and could blend almost anywhere. ""Sir?" was all Viggo said after closing the office door behind him.

"Status?" Carrizo asked as he opened the blinds to the single window.

"The girl will bring breakfast whenever you are ready. Jose is checking the mechanical condition of the vehicles. And three of your men arrived on horseback around 5am. They had a woman with them, she"s confined in casita three." Viggo might have had some sleep or not, Carrizo could never tell. The man's demeanor never wavered regardless of the circumstances. Crisp, respectful, unruffled and current on all relevant facts in all situations. Carrizo appreciated Viggo's multiple skills, his mid six figure salary was not an accident.

"Send the girl with plates now. I want the riders in this office in 20 minutes. Oh and make sure they bathe beforehand. Please… sit, eat with me. You can tell me about the woman they brought with them." Carrizo never turned from the view out the window. The sun glowed and promised another hot day. Carrizo and Viggo sat at the desk with the breakfast remains pushed to the side. A porcelain urn of café au lait sat between them and Carrizo waved a hand, indicating that Viggo should tell him about this woman.

"I looked in on her, she has a nasty cut on the face, a black eye, and perhaps a lump on the back of her head. I cannot be sure without touching her first. Gringo woman. Her horse is in the round pen. She's tied up and not going anywhere just yet. Tonio says that Miguel and El Gordo cooked up some scheme to kidnap a boy and hold him for ransom. Somehow this woman followed them and managed to free the child. El Gordo decided to keep her as a trade off of some sort. El Gordo has some sort of wound on his arm. Looks like part of that eagle tattoo is missing. Oh yes.. they do not know Miguel is dead." Viggo sat back in his chair and watched his boss carefully.

"Are you saying that these fools DID kidnap a boy, then lost him, then kidnapped an American woman who took the boy from them, and brought her HERE? All of this happened on my nephew Miguel's instructions?" Carrizo's tone was calm and pleasant, as if he were playing cards with his daughter. He sipped his coffee.

Viggo cleared his throat and continued, "There's more sir. Tonio says this woman is known to people here, she helped his sister last year. He says the boy was in her care when they took him. Her name is Tru Marcus." The name meant nothing to Viggo, but Carrizo froze. He knew the Marcus couple. It was his business to know about anyone in his territory that could be a problem or a help to him. Anyone living on the border with a reputation, good or bad, was someone he needed to have a little background intelligence on.

"So now I am to understand that these men, MY MEN, are holding a local woman hostage? Here, in my presence? A woman I have met and spoken with. A woman who has in fact, helped the family of an employee."" Carrizo rattled his cup as he placed it on the table. The twitch under his right eye began. "We will go to the casita and speak with her shortly. See to it she has food and medical care if she needs it, but keep her confined for now." Viggo nodded and rose to leave when Carrizo spoke again. ""One more thing. Find out where her husband is. I don't want a war over this Viggo. It's possible he was the one who killed Miguel."

Viggo held the door open for the fat man as he left the office. El Gordo slunk in and stood before the desk as Jose and the former camp boss had both done the night before. "El Gordo. You have been a busy man. Would you like to explain yourself?" Carrizo had his back turned and was once again admiring the mountain view from the window.

The fat man shuffled his feet and then whispered, ""Miguel senor. Miguel said we were to take one of the boys and they would pay in cash to get him back. He said it would be easy and you would be proud of his initiative.

That we would split the money and prove we are worth more to you than just sitting out here in the middle of nowhere for weeks, waiting on a shipment to leave."

Carrizo's eye tic was going in earnest now. "My nephew. This was all Miguel's idea? You do realize I cannot verify that. Miguel was killed yesterday. In the desert just south of the border with Tejas. It is my belief that he was killed by the husband of the woman you brought here. Do you think I am proud of my nephew, El Gordo?" With the last words, he turned his chair back to face the fat man and retrieve his coffee cup.

The fat man blanched and blinked rapidly, trying to wrap his mind around the colossal cluster fuck he now found himself standing in. Carrizo continued, "Miguel is dead. And his bodyguard. I have only YOUR word that these things happened the way you say. I can accept that. You have worked for me a number of years with no problems. But there is one simple question that no one seems to be able to answer. WHERE. IS. MY. MONEY?"

El Gordo stuttered. He backed up a step. His breathing sped up and his eyes widened. "Senor! We never took your money. Miguel sent it to pay the contact for the information about the boy. He said we would double what he paid."

Carrizo nodded in understanding. "Mistakes happen. People do things they regret and before you know it, it's too late. I have sympathy for a man in your position, Gordo, truly I do." He stood up and adjusted his tie slightly before walking to the office door. ""Send the other two in and please, address the situation with your arm… you are dripping blood on my carpet." Carrizo gestured disgustedly at the wet bandage around the fat man's forearm. The bite wound Azul had inflicted was starting to become infected.

By the time Viggo returned from checking on Tru, Carrizo had heard the same story from all three men. The short one had even gone so far as to say he thought he had seen the local sheriff when the woman had interfered. Jesus Christ, could these people be more incompetent? Carrizo's first impulse was to kill all three of them where they stood, but he could not leave the camp occupied by only the cook and Jose. And there was still the issue of his missing $72,000. It was a tiny sum in relation to his overall business expenses, but the principal of the matter was what counted. Theft by his own family? Disrespect at this level was intolerable. Kidnapping women and children was an act of such dishonor it made his stomach sour.

"Viggo. Let us take a walk." He donned a custom made white straw Panama hat as Viggo opened the door. Carrizo loved the desert, it cleared his head and made it easier to digest unfortunate news. He was postponing a call to his wife, telling her about Miguel's death would be a long drawn out affair and he just wasn't in the mood. There was wild bougainvillea in bloom next to the kitchens and hibiscus flowers in carefully tended plots along the path from the office to the landing pad. "I knew having a woman here would improve the aesthetics of the camp." Carrizo nodded to the flowers and Viggo agreed. He appreciated the little touches that added civility to the remote camp as much as his boss did. They strolled along and Viggo kept one eye out for trouble and an ear tuned to Carrizo.

"If I were the Marcus woman's husband, I would be here. Out there somewhere, waiting." Carrizo slipped a hand out of his pants pocket and waved at the canyon walls. "I would want to know how many men are on the grounds and an escape route. Then I would come in on foot, free my wife, kill everyone I could find and flee." The men had stopped walking in front of the casita Tru was being held in. Carrizo spent several long minutes, clearly visible to potential spying eyes, turning in a small circle, looking at the entire camp and the length of the canyon. Trying to see things from the perspective of an angry husband.

"Sir? If you think this man is already here, you should not be out in the open." Viggo stepped closer to Carrizo. "Do you want a search conducted?"

"No. I think instead, we will let him come Viggo. Take his wife, deal with matters in whatever way he chooses. It is about honor at this point. My own nephew has brought this on us. As I said earlier, I do not want a war here. I want my money back, I want our contact at the border eliminated and I want to be finished with this entire debacle." Carrizo slapped the bodyguard on the back and ducked inside the casita. The interior was dark and quiet. Tru was leaning against the back wall with her eyes closed. Carrizo took a long moment to study her and made note of the blackening eye with a grimace. He had killed women before in the line of business, but he had never condoned or allowed physical abuse of any woman. It was uncivilized and he refused to fall into that hole.

Carrizo kneeled next to Tru and softly touched her shoulder. She jerked back and her eyes flew open. "Aren't you dressed nice for the desert."

"I am afraid I did not have time to pack appropriately for this visit. Have you been given something for pain?" Carrizo was relieved that she was coherent and did not appear to have any broken bones.

Tru shrugged her shoulders and sat up a little straighter. "Your man there" nodding toward Viggo, "gave me some Tylenol and a coke earlier. The girl brought me some fruit. Of course since my hands are tied, I haven't exactly been able to enjoy the oranges.""

"I will send her back to help you eat. It is not my intention for you to suffer needlessly. However….. I think you must understand my position. I cannot simply turn you loose when I don't have all the facts for this situation." Carrizo gave her a cold smile and stood back up. " It seems my nephew Miguel made some…well, let's call them choices. And now you are here against your will. Miguel is dead. And I find I am missing $72,000."

He touched the oranges and soft bread in the bowl on the table. Picking up the water bottle and returning to Tru's side, he offered her a drink. "My hospitality is lacking on this day, I agree. You have my apologies. We will speak again Mrs. Marcus." He set the water back on the table, Tru had refused it. How humiliating was it to have this man in his designer suit offer her a bottle like a child?

"Surely you don't think I have your money? You seem smarter than that." Tru's tone was laced with bitterness.

Carrizo glanced down at her and smiled for real this time. "Madam. If you had my money, we would not be having this conversation. You would already be dead." He strolled to the doorway, tipped his hat at her and disappeared into the sunshine.

As he walked out of the casita, the scope of a rifle followed his every step. A kill shot was not out of the question, but Chris had no intention of shooting Jorge Carrizo. He did not want a war any more than Carrizo did. Chris noted the man's immaculate appearance, his bodyguard, the casual way they had stood in plain site before he entered the casita. He had seen the other men, the ones who had taken his wife, entering the office earlier. Something was off here, but he had no idea what. Chris hadn't seen Tru, but logic dictated she had to be in the casita Carrizo had just vacated.

Chris laid on his chest, the Scout rifle resting between his arms so he could use the scope to watch the camp.

The day was already heating up and his shirt was damp on his back with sweat. He rolled onto his back and packed up his rifle before crawling back off the canyon lip. He had a firm head count now, eight people including Carrizo, his bodyguard and the helicopter pilot. As far as Chris was concerned, the cook and the boy on the motorcycle were of no interest. The three men that dragged his wife to the camp were his primary targets. The pilot and bodyguard could be problems in a confrontation. Carrizo was off limits. Killing him would mean Chris and Tru spending the rest of their lives on the run.

He walked up to Whiskey and rubbed her nose. He had found a small valley behind the canyon with some shade and signs of water. He spent twenty minutes digging out a shallow depression under the roots of a cotton wood tree and water seeped up slowly, but steadily. It would provide enough for both him and his horse while they waited for nightfall.

10:30am

Anne stood in the cabin living room watching the Burgess family reunite. She had driven Jeff back to the cabin, arriving at the same time Janet did with the freshly repaired Suburban. Todd and David had packed all of their belongings while they waited. David left a note for Chris and Tru taped to the kitchen island.

"As much as I think I might enjoy your company normally, I'm going to have to say thank you and good-bye. I want my family out of here and safe at home." David shook Anne's hand and lugged two suitcases out to their car.

Janet was wiping her eyes with a tissue and holding onto Jeff at the same time. "Mooooommmm. I'm fine, let go so I can help Dad." The boy wiggled out from her grasp and darted out the door. Janet's face fell and she looked momentarily crushed.

"They are just boys Janet. It's nothing personal. I held on so tight to my boys that even I was sure I was suffocating them at times." Anne gave Janet a soft smile and offered her a fresh tissue. "I grew up an orphan in foster care. It makes you cling to the things that matter the most, the people that matter the most."

Janet sniffled and nodded in agreement. "Anne, I think you and I should have lunch one day. If you and your husband get a chance, you come see us in Austin. I promise…no criminals!"

"We would like that a bunch. Now go on home. Don't worry, I'll be sure the Marcuses know you are all safe and sound when they get back. Give me your number and I'll call you myself as soon at they get back." The women exchanged contact information, hugged one last time and the Burgess family drove away. Anne locked the cabin up and loaded two bags of horse feed from the barn into her own truck before she went back to town.

Chapter 25

11:30 AM

Hector walked out of the Houston International Bank with $6500 worth of traveler's checks. The duffle bag of cash was still secure in the floorboard of his little SUV when he pulled out of the parking lot. His meeting with the boat seller was at the Kemah Marina in an hour. The man had agreed to accept the traveler's checks for the final payment and to throw in a tank full of diesel so the boat would be ready to sail as soon as Hector was on board.

Hector was in a hurry when he rolled through the E-Z Pass line on the Sam Houston Toll Road. He exited onto I-45 South to the coast and arrived at Landry's Seafood Restaurant in Kemah exactly at 12:30. The seller was waiting at the entrance and gave Hector a hearty handshake. Over ice cold beers, Hector signed over the traveler's checks and the seller signed over the title documents to one "Jonathon Ramos". They asked the bartender to witness the signatures and transfers. Hector showed his new driver's license to the bartender for proof that he was Jonathon Ramos and then tipped her a twenty. Spending the Carrizo cash just came naturally to Hector.

Hector's step was easily ten pounds lighter when he returned to his vehicle. Assuming a fake identity was easy as pie when you had ready access to all the pertinent information. The Sheriff's name was simple and fairly common. Being the local county deputy had made a smooth operation out of obtaining a copy of the Sheriff's actual driver's license and social security number. The man's credit was fine and opening the bank account in Houston had taken mere minutes. Hector was confident that the entire paper trail would lead back to Sheriff Jonathon Ramos. By the time they sorted it out, Hector planned to be sailing the coast of Argentina. He pulled back onto the freeway, driving directly to the marina south west of Beaumont.

He made a fast stop at a sporting goods store to buy new snorkel gear, fishing reels and a couple of extra butane tanks for the stove on his boat. Carrizo's cash paid for all of it. Two hours later Hector parked his Ford Escape in a downtown garage and called a cab to take him to the marina. The fuel barge was just pulling back when Hector stepped aboard the ""Libertad", the Spanish word for "freedom". Hector had painted the name on the keel himself some months back. He waved at the barge pilot and stowed the bag of money and new supplies in the boat's small cabin. By the time he untied the Libertad and pushed back from the dock, he was whistling and sweating under the early afternoon sunshine as it reflected off the polished teak decking

Chapter 26

6:00pm

 Chris woke up from his nap on the ground. His back was stiff and his eyes and mouth felt gritty. Contrary to what the old TV shows would have you believe, using a saddle as a pillow was not comfortable. Whiskey was grazing nearby, the lead rope on her halter dragging the ground beside her. There was a puddle of cleanish water in the seep he had dug earlier and he scooped a bowl full of it out. He swished it around in his mouth and spat it back out. Then he washed his face with what was left. Better than nothing and his mind went to his wife, wondering if she even had access to a toilet down there. Around lunch time Chris had seen the cook take a covered plate into Tru's hut and the woman had stayed about thirty minutes with his wife. He was relieved to see Tru wasn't being starved or beaten, but he was puzzled about her treatment in general. It was pretty clear to him that Jorge Carrizo was in a holding pattern with regard to Tru, Chris didn't know why and that meant he couldn"t even guess what Carrizo's next move might be.

 Chris was back in his spot at the lip of the canyon wall, binoculars plastered to his eyes when the helicopter fired up. He saw the pilot inside as it elevated off the ground, but no passengers. He rolled back under the cover of the mesquite trees as the chopper lifted out of the canyon and turned south. "What the hell?" Chris looked back at the camp and saw the cook gathering eggs from a hen house and Jorge Carrizo leading a tall white Andalusian stallion out of a small barn. The horse's mane flowed from his arched neck down below the knees of his front legs in lustrous white waves. "Typical. Finest horse in 400 miles and he belongs to a drug dealer."" Chris narrowed his eyes and watched as Carrizo and the gorilla bodyguard mounted their horses and headed to the narrow road leading out of the camp. He continued to watch them until they turned a corner and headed west away from the camp entirely.

He waited a half hour for them to return. When they didn't he decided this was probably his best opportunity to make a move. Chris was sure there were just four men and the woman cook on the property. Not the best odds, but the element of surprise would help even things out. Chris was feeling a little jumpy. His second night out on the desert without a shower, a real meal or more than two hours of sleep in a row. Whiskey was half asleep with a hind foot cocked, her tail lazily sweeping at flies while she waited for Chris to finish checking his weapons. He put his rifle back in its scabbard, his pistol in his hip holster and the Condor knife on his belt. The last thing he did was check Whiskey's chest wound. There was a bit of swelling along the edges of the cut, but it had scabbed over well and was just a little tender to the touch. "Miss Whisk, I think it could be worse. You'll have to suck it up until we get home girl." Chris held a hard peppermint candy out for her and Whiskey gently took it from him, crunching as he got back in the saddle.

Dusk was starting to fall over the land when Chris tied Whiskey in the middle of a group of mesquite and ocotillo bushes a few hundred yards from the nearest camp building. There was a narrow goat trail leading out of the canyon and away from the gravel road. Chris hoped to be able to use this trail when he had Tru. They would go through the mountain rather than over the open desert and try to cross the Rio Grande a couple of miles further east than they had the night before. It was a longer trip distance wise, but would provide more cover in the event of a confrontation along the way. Chris glared up at the full moon beginning to glow overhead as he crept forward to the first hut, knife in his right hand, ready. A gun has it's place, but in close up, stealth work, the silence of the knife was the better option.

Chris tiptoed into the hut and saw a sleeping man on a hammock. It was one of the three cholos he had seen with Jeff at the shack in the desert. It took less than a minute for Chris to cut the man's throat and move on to the next casita while he gurgled and bled out in the hammock. The second casita was empty at first glance. It took a moment for Chris to realize a short man was sitting in a lawn chair in the corner, eyes closed and a bottle of tequila between his feet on the ground. Chris stared curiously for a moment at the man's hands, they were covered in Band-Aids. The man looked up at Chris as he started toward the chair. Not asleep. Chris stopped, thebloody knife against his pant leg. Toniotook hold of the tequila bottle as he stood and faced Chris. "Que pasa?"

Chris took a stalker stance, knees lightly bent, balanced on the balls of his feet, knife hand held slightly away from his body. "I no hable Spanish. What happened to your hands asshole?"

Tonio glanced at the knife and then down at his own torn up hands and said "Rope burns. La Senora's stallion.""

"Sounds about right." Chris took a step forward, keeping his eyes on Tonio's face.

Tonio figured he had one shot at making an escape. He flung the tequila bottle at Chris' head and bolted for the open doorway. The bottle narrowly missed Chris as he bounced to the right and ducked his head slightly. Tonio was two steps from the door when Chris stuck his leg out and brought Tonio to the ground face first. If Tonio had been slightly more sober, he might have kept his balance and not fallen. Chris had his knee pressed into the small of Tonio's back in seconds, his left hand pulling Tonio's head off the dirt as he reached around with his right hand and sliced Tonio's throat. "Two down, one to go." was all Chris thought when stood back up and dragged the body a few feet to the side and out of immediate view of a passerby.

From the doorway of Tonio's casita, Chris had a clear view of Azul in the round pen. Tru's saddle had been dragged outside of the pen and dropped near the gate. Azul still had his halter and dirty lead rope on and he was still filthy. Chris stood still and listened carefully. He could make out Azul chewing, a goat's bell chiming faintly on the other side of the camp, the blood dripping off his knife onto the dirt at his feet, but no people noise. He frowned and thought "Where is that fat fuck?"" Chris wanted all three of them dead before he and Tru rode out.

He darted out of the casita directly to the round pen gate. It only took seconds to open the gate, walk up to Azul and lead him through the gate. Chris swooped down with his left hand and grabbed the saddle horn, his right hand still holding the knife and Azul's lead rope. Chris didn"t hesitate, just walked right back into Tonio's hut. Azul's nostrils flared and he snorted at the scent of fresh blood, but he stood quietly as Chris saddled him in privacy. There was an old bridle in the hut, it looked like Tonio had been cleaning it before he started drinking in his lawn chair. Chris swapped the bridle for Azul's dirty halter and gave the stallion the last peppermint in his pocket. Tru's gun bag was attached to her saddle, but the gun itself was missing. Chris had a feeling he would find it when he found the fat man. Tru's Glock was too nice a weapon to ignore.

Tru opened her eyes and stared at the fat man in the doorway. He was leaning against the door frame cleaning his fingernails with a dirty pocket knife. A loose bandage was wrapped around the bite wound on his forearm. The skin below and above the bandage was red and swollen and his fingers looked puffy and painful. Tru watched him, silent behind the tape over her mouth. He had her gun tucked into the waistband of his pants. His beady eyes looked her up and down and Tru couldn't decide if he was comparing her to a juicy steak or considering what she could offer sexually.

El Gordo shifted his body weight against the doorway and scratched at the bandage with the pocket knife. The smell of stale sweat, beer, and rotting teeth floated toward Tru on a slight breeze. She wrinkled her nose in disgust and sat up straighter against the wall. She had some of her strength back, the girl had brought her a pretty decent meal earlier and helped her eat it. She had also helped Tru take more Excedrin and relieve herself. The goose egg on the back of her head hurt if she moved too quickly, but her face was down to a dull ache. Fat boy spoke. "El Jefe wants to send you back. Alive. His instructions are to take you back to the river tomorrow." He closed the pocket knife and slipped it into his pants pockets. Then rubbing the butt of her pistol in his waistband with his good hand, he continued "But I think that maybe accidents happen. Out in the desert… plans go wrong." El Gordo grinned at her and then waddled out into the night.

Tru thought to herself how much she would have liked to pistol whip the son of a bitch to death. She wanted to slowly peel that barbed wire tattoo off his neck with his own grime encrusted pocket knife. She had just begun to picture tying him out for the javelina to feast on when she heard a scuffle just outside her hut. Two loud thumps followed by a grunt and the beginning of a howl of pain. The howl was cut off almost instantly and Tru watched in amazement as the fat man's body fell backward in front of the entry and lay unmoving as blood gushed out of his severed neck arteries.

After leaving Azul with Whiskey, Chris had moved fast through the shadows to the casita his wife was being kept in. He came around the corner just as the fat man walked out of the casita. Chris instinctively reached down to grab the first thing he could find. It was a two foot length of steel pipe. Chris wasn't about to go hand to hand with a knife against this big man. The risk of being knocked off balance by the mass alone was too great. El Gordo looked up and saw Chris running directly at him, less than three feet away. Chris slammed the pipe into the man's bandaged forearm once, breaking the bones instantly. He swung the pipe again and took out El Gordo's right knee with a sickening crunch. As he fell to his other knee and sucked in air to begin screaming, Chris lunged a third time and slashed at his throat. His strike was so savage, he almost decapitated the man. Chris stepped into the bleeding body, snatched Tru's Glock from his waistband and tipped El Gordo's corpse backward with his boot. It landed along the threshold and Chris stepped over it on his way inside the hut.

A raised eyebrow greeted Chris as he ducked his head past the doorway and quickly looked around the tiny room. He moved in a half crouch, his light blue eyes searching the dim space for any movement other than the woman with the arched brow. Chris's blue jeans were covered in a layer of brown dust, his cowboy boots tracked bloody footprints with every step as he approached Tru.

Tru cleared her throat impatiently as she watched Chris make his way closer to her. The duct tape over her mouth prevented actual words. She rolled onto her left side and waggled her bound hands at him. Her thick red hair was caught in a disheveled pony tail, her clothes were filthy and damp with sweat. Tru had a shiner starting over the left eye and a cut on her cheekbone below it. Not her best look to be sure, but then again, it had not been a great day all the way around.

Chris stared hard at her face, his rage glimmering off him like a wave of heat. Dropping the pipe, he took her chin between his fingers, turning her head from side to side. Tru waggled her arms again, jerking both eyebrows up and down pointedly at the same time. "Sorry" he muttered and promptly started cutting the tape from her wrists with the bloody knife. As she stretched the cramps out of her fingers and gingerly rolled her shoulders forward, she cleared her throat loudly, looking him in the eye. Chris sighed deeply and gently pulled the tape from her mouth.

"Where the HELL have you been? Piddle around much?" Tru's tone was light, teasing almost. Chris did not look up as he started slicing at the duct tape on her ankles. "You do understand why a man would be tempted to leave your mouth gagged, right?" he calmly asked.

""Ready to go?" Once her ankles were free, he darted back to the doorway, motioning behind him for her to come on. She stood up slowly, testing her ankles' ability to bear weight properly before she followed hris.

They stood in silence near the doorway, the moonlight beginning to reflect off the dead man lying at the threshold, blood pooling alongside his severed throat. Chris turned with his back against the wall and reached behind him to pull a pistol from the small of his back. He handed it butt first to Tru and patted the holster on his hip to reassure that his own weapon was where he could get to it. "Thank you!" Tru smiled at him as she chambered a round in the Glock 45 caliber pistol and balanced it in her right hand. It felt comfortable. It felt right to be armed again.

"Hey. Where is your engagement ring?" Chris nodded to her left hand.

"You find me on the floor, bound and gagged in the middle of nowhere and THAT is what you're worried about?"

"It was an expensive emerald." he grunted, his eyes once again looking out the doorway of the hut.

"Big too. I swallowed it. We'll see it in a couple of days I imagine." Tru was right behind him, staring outside over his shoulder.

"All right honey. Follow me and stay quiet. We leave this hut, turn left for about 100 feet to that big bunch of ocotillo plants. Straight from there about a football field length and you'll see the horses. If we get into a fire fight you RUN. Understand?"

Tru took a deep breath to steady her nerves and then she noticed the grin on Chris' face. He casually stepped over the very fat dead guy in the doorway and into the evening beyond.

It was hot, no breeze moved the heat and the scent of fresh blood hung in the air. Goats could be heard in the distance and a hoot owl further away. No human noises were heard as Tru and Chris edged their way out of the hut and along the side to a path illuminated by moonlight. Tru jumped slightly as the thin metal roof of the hut creaked when a lizard darted over it. Chris didn"t even acknowledge the sound, his eyes darting from side to side as he led his wife through the ramshackle collection of dirt casitas. His immediate goal was to get to the goat trail where he had left their two horses without being shot in the process.

They paused just beyond the perimeter in a group of ocotillo plants and took stock of the situation. Tru's hand was wrapped easily around her Glock. Chris brushed a finger over the line of her jaw and she whispered "I never doubted you, you know." He just winked at her. She could hear the soft snuffling noises of their horses now. She started off in that direction, Chris right behind her, splitting his attention to the path behind them. Watching for pursuers. Watching to see if anyone was still alive who could pursue them. Being a killer did not faze him in the least. His wife or these sleazebags? That choice was so simple he gave it no thought at all. Slitting their throats had taken no more emotional toll than buttering a biscuit at his breakfast table. There had to be others out there somewhere and they would be looking for payback. That thought did worry Chris. They had a two day ride through the harsh terrain of the Chihuahuan desert back to Texas. Alone they could make it with a minimum of drama, but chased by thugs intent on vengeance? Well.... that presented a problem

    Tru wrapped her arms around Azul's neck before climbing into the saddle. Chris led the way back up the goat trail and out of the canyon. Once the camp was behind them and almost invisible, they stopped and Chris handed her a bottle of water. "That seem too easy to you?"

    "Definitely. I heard the helicopter leave earlier, but I don't know who was on it." Tru passed the water back to Chris and slipped her Glock back into its travel bag.

    "I watched it with the binoculars and it was just the pilot. Carrizo and his gorilla went out on horseback maybe 35 minutes before I reached you."

    "Viggo. The gorilla's name is Viggo. He brought me some pain pills and water this morning. Oddly enough, he was terribly polite."

    "Don't start with me Tru." Chris warned, "If I get the chance, I'll put a bullet in his head. I don't give a shit how polite he is." He touched Whiskey's sides with his heels and began to move on down the path. Tru followed him. She just let him mutter under his breath about women being too soft hearted and not understanding the difference between a rabid dog wearing a pretty collar and an actual pet. She knew that Chris understood she did not expect him to forgive these people. The adrenaline had him wound up, snappish and she took no offense.

    They rode in silence at a quick trot for another twenty minutes, putting some distance between themselves and the camp. The mountain trail was beginning to widen and even out as they descended back to the desert floor further east than the gravel road entry into the box canyon. Tru pushed Azul up alongside Whiskey and said "Honey. I know we're in a hurry here, but I need to take something for my headache."

Chris looked over at her and his expression softened. He could see the bump on the back of her head and he wanted to wrap her up in their bed with a down comforter and pillows. Just at the edge of the desert was a limestone overhang on the side of the mountain. Not a cave, but a semi enclosed space where they could rest a bit without being out in the open. It went against his gut instinct to stop at all, but he knew if Tru passed out they would be screwed ten ways from Sunday.

Chapter 27

7:00pm

Sheriff Ramos had spent almost the entire day in his office on the phone and the computer. Searching for Hector. He had finally gone home at 4pm in need of sleep. Anne was asleep on top of the covers when he laid down next to her. She had delivered Jeff safely to the Burgess family earlier in the morning and then stopped by Jonathon's office with take out sandwiches at lunch time. Tru's mare Rose was still ensconced in the Ramos barn. Anne had seen to the care of both horses again in late afternoon and neither were any worse for wear and recovering nicely. There still had been no word from the Marcuses.

Ramos got up from his nap and tried to make up his mind about what to do next. He had put a "be on the lookout" for Hector's Ford Escape notice to Texas DPS and the Galveston police department on a hunch. It had taken the Houston International Bank four hours to respond to his official, but warrant-less request for information about the account number on the deposit receipt found in Hector's house. The bank had faxed over a basic form listing the account owner's name, address, current balance and a letter stating that any further information would have to come from a court order. Reading that fax was what had convinced Ramos it was time to go home and get some sleep. The account was in his name and Hector's address with a current balance of $126,455. The Sheriff's blood pressure rose so fast and so high, his entire face went red and his pulse was plainly visible in every vein on his neck. Rage. Pure, unadulterated homicidal rage. Now, four hours later, he was still pissed off, but calmer. There was no doubt that Hector would be making a withdrawal of some sort from the Houston bank. No man would just walk away from a hundred thousand dollars. Watching that account and tracking the money would eventually lead to the deputy, but Ramos really did not want to wait that long. As he changed into civilian clothes, Ramos realized he sort of wished Chris Marcus were there to knock this around with.

"Anne, I think I'm going to take a run up to Houston in the morning." Ramos sat down at the kitchen table with his wife and served a heap of lasagna onto his plate. "Hector is going to want that money and I want to be close to it. My gut tells me he won"t wait for things to cool off."

Anne regarded her husband carefully and in a measured voice, she said "Are you really sure you want to deal with this…personally? Why don't you call the Texas Rangers and let them investigate it. They can find Hector and arrest him. Your hands stay clean that way Jonathon." She looked down at her plate and waited for his reply. She rarely got involved with his professional issues, but this situation seemed to require some distance. She knew how important his reputation was and Hector's betrayal was a direct insult to that pristine reputation.

"Anne, I don't want to involve outsiders. I know where that money came from and why. Hell I can even prove it. What I can't do is allow that BOY," Jonathon almost spat the words. ""to walk on top of me like this without facing me directly."

"Will you at least wait until the Marcuses get back? Isn't their safety still a concern here?" Anne walked to the refrigerator and pulled out a fresh cherry pie. She set it on the table and Jonathon began slicing it.

"Of course. Ah..Hell. Honey, I'm just tired. I don't know what I'm going to do yet. But I can tell you that little piss ant will not get away and he will NOT get that cash." Jonathon passed her a piece of pie with a tight smile.

Anne suddenly froze with the fork midway to her mouth and whispered "Technically that money belongs to YOU."

Their eyes met and both cracked up laughing. They laughed until tears flowed down their faces and Anne had the hiccups. The sheriff put his chin in one hand and leaned forward with his elbow perched on the dining table. "We could take that cruise around the Greek islands."

Anne took his hand in hers and tipped her head toward the bedroom, "We could just buy a bigger bed." The Ramoses spent the rest of the evening behind closed doors and under the covers.

8:00pm

Chris and Tru were moving again. She had taken four more Excedrin for the headache and glugged down half the Dr Pepper Chris had thought to bring for her when he left the cabin. She certainly felt better with some sugar in her system and Chris commented that she looked better too. They were alternating between walking and trotting on another rock strewn goat trail on the edge of the mountain. It was too dark to safely go any faster unless they moved onto the open desert. Chris did not want to do that just yet. They caught each other up on what had happened as they traveled. Tru was relieved that Jeff had last been seen in the custody of Sheriff Ramos and she demanded that they stop so she could give Whiskey's wound a once over for herself. Chris humored her, they both knew he had done all the right things to treat the mare, but Tru would always double check his work with the horses. It was just her thing. Chris did the same thing when she swore up and down the oil in the truck was fine or that the Christmas lights all worked. They tried to figure out why Jeff had been snatched and if Carrizo was actually involved or not and who had his missing money.

They stopped the horses at a cross roads in the trail. Straight would take them up a cliff rise and give them a long distance view of the terrain surrounding them. The path to the left followed a currently dry creek bed into an arroyo heading South. They both jumped like scalded cats when a loud electronic double beep sounded in Chris' pocket. It was Miguel's phone. "What the hell?" Chris stared at the phone when the double beep sounded again. Tru shrugged and Chris answered it. Tru was searching her own pockets for her Blackberry. It had no signal when she found it. Then it dawned on her that the stolen phone was also a push to talk radio model.

"Yes!" Chris spoke into the dead man's phone like he owned it.

The voice on the other end was modulated and structured from years spent in a British boarding school, yet still carried a soft Mexican accent. "I am assuming you are Christopher Marcus?"

"I am." Chris' voice hardened a notch and he met Tru's eyes. She turned Azul so that their horses were standing head to tail and both of them could see anyone coming up the trail from either direction.

"Excellent. My name is Jorge Carrizo and I believe you have answered my nephew's cellular telephone." Carrizo's tone was formal, polite even and betraying none of his irritation.

"Senor Carrizo. It was his phone."" Chris mouthed "Carrizo himself" to Tru. She rolled her eyes of course, who else would it be?

"It is my understanding that my nephew is dead? May I assume this was at your hand?"

"He is. I killed him, but you already know that and you know why." Chris knew he was walking a tight rope with this man. It was one thing to take action in the immediacy of the moment, but there was always a price later. The only question was how much and how painful it would be.

Carrizo sighed before he continued. "You have caused me no small amount of inconvenience tonight Mr. Marcus. And my nephew, well he has been a thorn in my side for some months now. To be honest, I would not care that you killed him except for one small detail."

"What detail would that be?" Chris was making a distinct effort to keep his own voice level. He never minded picking a fight, but he did try to avoid the fights he had no prayer of winning.

"It turns out that the boy was carrying $72,000 of my money. I would very much like that money back."

Chris edged Whiskey forward a few feet on the trail. Tru stayed put and listened. "I wish you luck with that. I want to get the hell home without further damage to my wife or my horses. If I knew where your cash was, I would tell you. I don't, so here's what I'll tell you instead...." Tru cringed, she knew how Chris normally finished that sentence, something along the lines of fuck you. She snapped her fingers to get his attention and drew a line over her own throat and whispered ""CAREFUL".

"Mr. Marcus? Are you still there?" Carrizo's tone had hardened a bit while he waited for Chris finish.

Chris ground his teeth and heeded his wife's warning. "I don't want a problem between you and me. What will it take for you to let us leave?" Tru was looking all around with the binoculars from her gun bag. If that phone was a two way radio, it had a limited range and that meant Carrizo and Viggo had to be nearby.

"I have no intention of stopping you. It was never my wish to have you here in the first place. I think we can agree that you have specific knowledge of my distribution facility and I, in turn, have specific knowledge of at least five murders committed by you. In Mexico. None of these things bears repeating to outsiders." Carrizo waited patiently for Chris to weigh his words.

A veiled threat is as potent as a direct one. ""Silence on both sides. Your business operations are the least of my concerns. I assume my cabin won't be burned to the ground at some point in the future?" Chris relaxed a bit in his saddle and Tru shot him a thumbs up.

Carrizo smiled on the other end. A fine example of having weighed all the possible outcomes of a given situation and knowing what the results would be before he acted. "Certainly not. I am not a savage Mr. Marcus. Perhaps in the future, we can share a drink and discuss horseflesh. We'll meet soon. Buenos noches." The line went dead in Chris" ear.

He and Tru sat there in silence for a long couple of minutes, staring at each other and the trail. Finally Azul stamped his feet and tossed his head. "We're lollygagging" Tru muttered as she let Azul trot onto the arroyo path. Chris and Whiskey followed.

Jorge Carrizo was a curious man. He had sent his chopper back to Chihuahua to retrieve replacements for the three men who had brought Tru Marcus to the mountain camp. He knew Chris could not miss seeing it leave and he wondered if Chris would see it as an opportunity to sweep down and rescue his wife. So he had taken Viggo on his own horses out for the evening. Once outside of the compound, they doubled back to a small tunnel blasted into the caliche that made up parts of the canyon wall. Carrizo had had the tunnel excavated years ago as an escape route of last resort. He and Viggo sat just inside the opening overlooking the camp and watched Chris make his calculated way through the camp. Viggo had wanted to take a vehicle and follow the couple, but Carrizo felt like riding instead. They took a ridge path on the high side of the mountain until it dead ended overlooking the desert below and the goat trail along the mountain's base. When Chris and Tru appeared on the goat trail, Carrizo pulled out his cell phone and paged Miguel's phone. He smiled when Chris answered it.

Once the conversation was over, Carrizo replaced his phone in his shirt pocket and looked at his bodyguard. "I think perhaps we have some housecleaning to attend Viggo."

Chapter 28

Dawn

Their third day away from home dawned bright and promised to be baking hot and dry. Chris and Tru had stopped after midnight and made camp. The horses were tired, but Tru was almost done in. Chris found them a sheltered spot in an arroyo with an overhang and two small cotton wood trees. While he was digging out another water seep between the tree roots, Tru cut two barrel cactus open and sliced the soft, spongy insides. She gathered mesquite beans from the closest trees and offered a mix of both to each of their horses. It wasn't the hay and grain they would have had at home, but combined with what little grazing was available, the concoction offered protein, some sugar and moisture. Both horses ignored the cactus, there were still small patches of scrub grass available to eat. The cactus flesh could be sucked for moisture in a pinch, but Chris and Tru had not reached that point just yet. They still had a full bottle of water, half of Tru's Dr Pepper left and whatever water accrued in the seep after the horses had their fill.

Chris debated whether to have a fire or not. When he took a closer look at Tru's pale face, he decided to take Jorge Carrizo at his word that they were free to leave unmolested. After setting some rocks in a two foot circle, he gathered several fallen mesquite branches and some dry grass for kindling. Tru tossed him one of the 9-volt batteries and some steel wool as a fire starter before she lay down and closed her eyes. Her face was definitely swelling under her left eye and the headache was almost constant. Chris curled up beside her and wrapped his arms around her next to the fire.

The morning's first light was a welcome reprieve from the cold of the night. The fire had burned out and the horses were some distance away down the arroyo grazing, but they had not been accosted by anymore of Carrizo's men while they slept. Dawn also brought the realization that Tru needed a doctor. Sooner rather than later. The goose egg on the back of her head hadn"t shrunk in the night and her eye was almost swollen shut. The sight of it made Chris want to kill El Gordo all over again. Tru was lucid and able to focus mentally, but she was tired and hungry. So was Chris and when he mentioned this fact to her, she narrowed her one good eye at him and said "Yes, but where is YOUR concussion?" With a sigh he offered her the last pack of M&Ms in his saddle bag. She shook out half in her palm and gave the rest back to him.

They got a slower start than Chris would have liked, even the horses were grumpy. Azul showed his teeth to Chris when he tightened the cinch on his saddle. Whiskey pawed the ground with irritation when she was saddled, but did not offer to bite anyone. "You always did have better manners than dickhead." Chris whispered to her and rubbed her nose.

Tru snorted and held her hand out to Azul without even looking at the horse. Who then politely and gently lipped a single M&M from her palm. "He just wanted a candy first Chris."

"The day I buy a horse dinner and a movie before a ride, Hell will freeze." He kicked his mare into a light trot while Tru tried not to laugh. Her head hurt too much for actual laughter.

They crossed the Rio Grande at noon. Azul was walking slowly and deliberately, placing each foot carefully. If Whiskey got too close, his ears would lay flat on his head as a warning. Tru was drooping precariously in the saddle, the reins held loosely between two fingers and she looked like she had been in a car wreck. Her eye was almost entirely black and swollen totally shut. The cut under her eye was covered with a Band aid and antibiotic cream beneath, but still glowed red at the edges. The heat, constant movement and lack of real food had combined with the knot on her head to leave her in a deep fog. She was dehydrated and weak. Chris was concerned she might not actually be able to get home.

"Honey. HONEY!" Chris had to holler before Tru registered that he was speaking to her. "Stop. I'm going to get you down for a bit before you fall off." Tru didn't say a word, just tugged on Azul's reins and he stopped instantly. She was limp when Chris pulled her from the saddle and helped her sit on the riverbank grass under a salt cedar tree. He got her to drink some water, but the Excedrin was long gone.

"Tru. TRUDY!!" Chris was yelling again and she smiled at him drowsily. "Stay here baby. I'll be back. We need help. Just don't move from this spot." He leaned forward and kissed her on the mouth. He loosened Azul's cinch and left his reins dragging, ground tying him next to Tru. Then he got back on Whiskey and kicked her into a full gallop into Texas. He rode for the first mesa he could see at top speed. Whiskey was still sliding to a full stop when Chris began dialing the sheriff's office on Miguel's cell phone. The phone had one bar of reception and there was no higher ground nearby.

The phone rang three times before Ramos answered and the line was full of static. "Jonathon. It's Chris Marcus. I have Tru and she's hurt. Pick us up at the river. Roughly three miles east from last night."

"Chris? I can barely hear you. Say again where are you?" Ramos was already straightening his Stetson and grabbing his truck keys.

"Three miles east of last night. She's got a concussion and is out of it. Come get her right now man." The connection was lost. "GODDAMN TELCEL!" Chris shouted and slammed the phone against the saddle horn in frustration. He jerked Whiskey's head back toward the river and sent her into a hard gallop back to his wife.

12:45pm

Sheriff Ramos jammed the county truck into four wheel drive and tore over the desert faster than he should, bouncing over rocks and pot holes. A thrashed and flattened line of creosote and sage bushes made a wake behind the truck. Anne held on to the "oh shit" grab handle on the passenger door frame and prayed. She had been sitting in the office helping her husband do internet searches for any trace of Hector. They had grabbed the first aid kit, water and the picnic basket Anne had brought with her.

Jonathon starting laying on the horn when he thought they were in the general vicinity of the Marcuses. A half mile later, horn blaring and the rear tires skidding sideways in the sand, a dark bay horse shot out of the trees along the river bed in front of them. Jonathon slammed on the brakes and whipped the wheel to the left to avoid running right into the horse. Chris waved both arms frantically, spun his horse in a tight pirouette and rode back the way he had come. Sheriff Ramos parked the truck on the edge of the tree line and both of them ran the rest of the way.

"Jesus Christ! Oh Tru…. Come on you men, get her to the truck." Anne took one look at Tru's face and went directly into nurse mode. She ran back to the truck ahead of them and laid out the first aid gear and turned the air conditioner on high. Chris and Jonathon carried Tru between them and set her in the back seat. Anne immediately began issuing instructions while she soaked a rag with water to wash Tru's face off. "Jonathon, get on the radio and call for a medivac chopper to meet us on the highway. Then start driving. I'll take of things back here. Chris you get your horses to our house. Do you know the way?"

Chris said "I do. I need to go with her."" "No. We do things my way from here on out.

You two were out on a moonlight ride, got attacked, chased and lost. We clear?"" This was the Sheriff talking now. His lone star badge glinted in the sun on his chest. This was the Sheriff who made the rules on

THIS side of the Rio Grande. Chris didn't take his eyes off Tru and Anne, but he relented and backed away so Anne could shut the truck door. Sheriff Ramos clamped a hand on Chris' shoulder briefly and got in the driver's seat. Chris walked back to his horses, mounted Whiskey, took Azul's reins in his left hand began the six mile trek to the Ramos house. Alone.

Chapter 29

Four Days Later

Tru spent three days in the hospital in Alpine. She had an ugly concussion, but the doctors did not expect any lingering ill effects. X-rays revealed a tiny hairline fracture in her upper cheekbone where El Gordo's boot had made contact. She also had five stitches and a future scar under her eye. She had a mild case of heat stroke as a bonus present and spent the first two days almost entirely asleep with iv fluids, antibiotics and painkillers. When she awoke on the third day Chris was asleep in a chair next to her bed and there four vases of flowers on the window sill next to him. The cards from each were on the bedside table with an unopened Dr Pepper. Tru drank the first sip with a physical shiver of pleasure and no nausea for the first time since she had been admitted.

She picked up the flower cards and smiled when she saw the one from Janet and David Burgess and the handwritten note suggesting that perhaps the next get together should be at their home in Austin. They had sent a bouquet of blue hydrangea blooms. The next two were from Chris and the Ramos couple. Chris had brought lovely Asiatic Lilies surrounding three yellow roses. The yellow rose of Texas was her favorite. Her husband never forgot. Anne and Jonathon had sent pink calla lilies.

The last card was larger than the others and was sealed in a matching envelope. Opening it released a faint scent of cinnamon. She pulled out a heavy, champagne colored linen card. In beautiful, crisp fountain pen script was written

"It is my wish that you accept these yellow roses as a gesture of my good will and esteem for you. Until we meet again, Jorge."

There they were. At the far end of the window sill, set apart from the others. Three dozen of the most beautiful yellow roses she had ever seen. Arranged artfully in what had to be a Lalique crystal vase. "Good grief" Tru muttered.

Chris was awake the instant he heard her voice. He smiled at her and looked at the card still in her hand. "Ol' Carrizo likes to show off, doesn't he?" Chris nodded toward the Carrizo flowers.

"Think he'll pick up this hospital bill? As a gesture of his 'good will"?" Tru grinned at Chris and then wrinkled her nose. "Is that you or me that smells so bad?"

Chris looked indignant and said "I've been sleeping here for three nights. I haven't even had time to go to the cabin!"

Tru gave him one of those 'wife' looks that men get when they are preaching to the wrong choir, "I can SEE the shower from here. It's a PRIVATE room. Go get in it already!""

Chris and Tru spent the next day at the cabin, recovering. Chris had retrieved their horses from the sheriff's barn. Whiskey had healed faster than Tru. Chris called the kennel and made arrangements for their dogs to stay another few days and let the workers at their farm know they were delayed coming home. Tru slept most of the day and all night. Chris sat up watching her sleep and waiting for the other shoe to drop.

Two days after bring released from the hospital, Tru got up feeling pretty close to normal again. She took a shower, fed her horses and made bacon and egg breakfast sandwiches. Chris was still asleep when she brought him his sandwich and a mug of coffee. They spent the morning talking and getting intimately reacquainted.

Around 4 in the afternoon, they were perched in the rocking chairs on the cabin's porch with martinis in old fashioned, thin stemmed shallow glasses. Chris's glass was actually full of ginger ale. He rarely drank alcohol of any kind, but he found his wife endlessly amusing when she got tipsy. Chris nodded his head toward their road and a plume of dust floating above it. "Company coming. Dollar says it's the Sheriff.""

Tru slid her bare feet back into her loafers and leaned forward in her chair. "You don't think he means to charge you for what happened over there, do you?"

"Guess we'll find out. Stay here, I'll meet him." Chris walked down the front steps as the Sheriff's county truck pulled up and parked. Sheriff Ramos stepped down and the two men shook hands. Anne waved to Tru as she disentangled herself from the passenger side seatbelt.

When everyone was settled on the porch and had a drink in their hands, Ramos began. "I filed an official report about the attack on Trudy the night you were out for a ride. Border patrol says they found signs of other horsemen in the vicinity, but no one has been arrested or even questioned. Without a solid description of the perpetrators, there just isn't much to go on." The Sheriff looked at each one of them for a long moment when he finished.

Anne nodded and said "It was just darn lucky we happened to be in the area when you called for help. You might have been lost out there for days."

Chris and Tru shared a glance and Chris said ""I appreciate all your help. Both of you. I understand if you need to drop the investigation into who "attacked" us. After all, we didn"t get a good look at any of them and it was dark."

Tru almost choked on her drink, trying not to laugh. The Sheriff stared hard at her and she got it together fast. "Now that the official news has been shared, I think we need to take a walk and deal with the personal stuff." Ramos offered his hand to Tru and she accepted the help standing up graciously.

The foursome strolled into the barn where the horses were casually munching hay. "Jonathon, can I assume you don't intend to charge my husband with murder?" Tru was never good at subtly beating around a bush. She preferred the chain saw method. Anne grinned, but Chris and Jonathon both cringed. It's one thing to acknowledge the unspoken problem, but neither man was interested in bludgeoning it out in the open. ""I know…I know. We shouldn't even be talking about it, but I also need to know for sure what we're all doing here." Tru shrugged her shoulders and ran a hand through her hair.

The Sheriff sighed, pushing his Stetson to the back of his head and wiping his brow with a handkerchief. "I don't reckon I need to charge him with anything Tru. I saw what I saw and I was out of my jurisdiction anyway. Looked to me as if it was a mercy killing and right now we…I have other problems."

"Hector?" Chris asked quietly and opened the tack room door. Everyone trooped in and took a seat on the two chairs or tack trunks in the room.

"Hector." Ramos sat heavily on a trunk. "That son of a bitch has woven a nest of snakes here. He was taking money from Carrizo for the last two years. To the tune of over $100,000. He set up the whole kidnapping of the kid. He set up a paper trail for the bribes that leads directly back to me. And he's literally in the wind. I believe he"s gotten a boat of some sort and set sail."

Chris whistled and leaned against the tack room window shaking his head. "You had no idea?"

"Hell if I had thought he was up to no good, none of this would have ever happened." Anne placed a hand over Jonathon's and gave it a soft squeeze. "I'm asking a favor of you here, Chris. We need to hunt him down."

"Your personal ethics limit the actions you can take when you find him? Is that why you want me to help you?" Chris' tone was slightly bitter. "I owe you, no question, but I want all of us to understand what you're asking me to do here."

"Chris…" Tru's tone was soft and soothing.

"Dammit Tru. Don't "Chris" me. I don't mind dirty work, but it needs to be even ground." Chris didn't raise his voice and his eyes never left the Sheriff.

The conversation came to an abrupt halt at the sound of a vehicle near the cabin. Chris looked out the tack room window behind him and said "Any of you care to guess who drives a black Range Rover? With a chauffer?"

Chapter 30

Tru and Chris walked directly to the front of the cabin. Sheriff Ramos and Anne followed more slowly, the Sheriff unsnapped his pistol holster as he walked a step in front of his wife. The chauffer walked to the rear passenger door and held it open as Viggo exited the vehicle. He had a handgun openly showing in a shoulder holster under his sport coat. Viggo stood at his full 6" 6" height and turned in a full circle surveying the immediate area. He nodded his head in Chris and Tru's direction and then stepped back from the car door.

Senor Jorge Carrizo stepped out of the back seat behind Viggo. He was dressed casually in a tailored pair of black cotton pants, a grey button down cotton shirt, black crocodile loafers that cost as much as some people earn in a year, and a summer weight herringbone sport coat left open. No tie, hat or cufflinks today. His only adornment was a custom Rolex watch. It was almost as if he had made a concerted effort to appear relaxed and friendly. He glanced at the cabin for a long moment before acknowledging the four people staring at him.

"Ah. I am so glad to find you all together. It will save me a trip into town Sheriff." Carrizo smiled at Ramos as Viggo closed the car door behind him. "We have a great deal to talk about I think."

The Sheriff tilted his head slightly and replied. ""Mr. Carrizo. I can't say it's a pleasure exactly." Anne inhaled sharply at his rudeness, but said nothing.

"Mr. Carrizo, why are you here?" Tru took a step forward to face him directly. She wanted him to see the black eye that was just beginning to fade to yellow.

Viggo cleared his throat behind his boss and crossed his arms over his chest. Not a casual stance, one meant to allow him fast access to his weapon if the situation demanded. "Senora Marcus I see you have made a strong recovery from your....well, unfortunate ordeal." Carrizo stared unflinchingly at her eye. "I trust you received the flowers I sent?"

"I would have sent a thank you note, but of course, there is no mailing address for your torture center." Tru was snarky, but this man had appeared uninvited on HER territory this time.

Carrizo took no visible offense, chuckling lightly and saying, "Touche madam. Now if you don't mind, is there somewhere less dusty and cooler where we can speak? There are a number of things the five of us must come to some agreement on."

Chris stepped between Carrizo and Tru, Viggo once again shifting position and clearing his throat. "Didn't you and I already come to an agreement once? I don't know what the Hell kind of business you think we have together."

Sheriff Ramos spoke before Carrizo could reply. ""Chris, umm, why don't we take this inside the house. I know Anne could use a glass of tea." Anne glanced at him with surprise, why was he dragging HER into this? She poked him in the small of his back just to make sure he knew they would have a conversation about this later. "Besides, it's going to be dark soon." Neither Chris nor the Sheriff wanted to be standing around outside with this man in the dark.

Carrizo smiled and gestured to his Range Rover with one hand, "I keep a fully stocked bar in the back if you prefer something stronger?"

Tru couldn't help it, she laughed out loud and said "Of course you do. Good grief, come on in the house. If we don't, he'll have Viggo here build a teepee out of popsicle sticks and bubblegum." Viggo suppressed a grin behind a fake cough.

"I would never chew bubble gum. We carry a tube of super glue with the spare tire." Carrizo sounded genuinely amused. He found he actually liked the Marcus woman, had a little respect for her really. She had withstood mistreatment by his people, an incredibly difficult journey back home and a three day stay in the hospital as a result, yet she was still willing to stand her ground with him. She would probably make a fine camp boss in another life.

Chris sighed and made a mental note to talk to his wife about creating a list of future unwelcome house guests. He turned his back to Carrizo and led the way through the front door. Chris and Tru entered first, followed by Carrizo and Viggo. Anne and the Sheriff brought up the rear. The Sheriff stopped once and took a look around the property, noting a pair of men standing next to a second Range Rover at the end of the driveway. One facing the cabin and the other at the back of the vehicle, facing any possible incoming traffic. Both men carried shotguns openly and the chauffer had pulled out a rifle of his own as he took up a post near the porch, facing the road.

Chris and Viggo remained standing at opposite ends of the living room, every one else sat. "I suppose I should start with an apology. To all four of you. As I am sure you know this situation was not of my making. I am not in the business of kidnapping women and children and I am not in the habit of doing anything so…sloppily." Carrizo met each of their eyes for emphasis as he spoke. His tone was soft and friendly, he could have been apologizing for stepping

on the cat's tail.

"So you've said before." Chris was holding back his anger by a string.

"Perhaps." Carrizo lazily turned his way, pulling his coat off at the same time. Viggo stepped forward and took the coat from his boss, folded it carefully over one arm and returned to the background. "I have new information that I think you will find interesting. Especially you Sheriff."

Sheriff Ramos said nothing. He had learned long ago to let a suspect tell you what he wants to tell you in his own time. Pressure has it's place, but sometimes silence will compel the other person to fill it. Clearly Carrizo knew this trick as he said nothing further. Anne couldn"t stand it though. "What information?"

Carrizo sat back into the leather arm chair, straightened the pleat in his pants and crossed his legs elegantly. "About your former man, Hector Williams. I believe I know where he is. Surely this is information you can use?"

Sheriff Ramos eyed Carrizo with distrust. "Why would you have information about Hector?"

" Because he has something of mine that does not belong to him. I very much want it back. The man has, in a way, harmed each of us in this room. I am pleased to share what I know with you." Carrizo turned his head toward Tru and continued, "Might I beg of you a cup of coffee?"

Tru was embarrassed by her own lack of courtesy and said "Of course. Anyone else want a cup? Viggo?" The big man gave her a tight smile and shook his head.

Chris wasn't sure who he wanted to snap at his wife for treating these people like guests or Viggo for declining her offer. Instead he sat on his coffee table directly in front of Carrizo. "I"ll give you this, you have got a pair of brass balls on you Carrizo." Viggo took a single step closer to his boss's side. Carrizo silently held up a hand and Viggo froze. Chris never broke eye contact with Carrizo and continued, "I don't give a damn about your lost money. I don't give a damn about Hector. I have already taken care of the problems that concerned me. As you well know. And yet here you sit. Why?"

"Mr. Marcus you were dishonored and your wife suffered. I was dishonored and robbed. Sheriff Ramos was dishonored and in fact will face criminal charges when this situation comes to light. He will face ruination as a result of Hector's actions and because of the way you handled your problem in Mexico. Normally, I would seek redress privately and let the good Sheriff sink." Carrizo politely accepted the mug Tru offered him.

"Thanks." Sheriff Ramos wasn"t bitter, but the sarcasm was clear. "I have been sorting the paper and electronic trail for Hector for a week. I know full well what the piss ant has done. I can document that I was not involved."

"Can you? Are you entirely sure? From where I sit, you could possibly come away from this without charges, but also without your pension." Carrizo's tone was matter of fact. "My sources indicate that Hector has left an account with $100,000 in your name in Houston. Further more, he has purchased a boat in your name. As of this morning, Hector was no longer in US waters. Additionally, you will find that tonight an additional incentive of $50,000 has been deposited in the Houston account."

The Sheriff's face turned an alarming shade of red. "You son of a bitch." Viggo shifted position quietly behind Carrizo's head, allowing his jacket to open a hair and reveal his still holstered weapon.

"As I said earlier, it is not my intention to cause you harm. However, I believe we all have compelling reasons to help one another. Call it what you like, but I think if we work together, this little problem can be taken care of. Without the need for outside…talent."

Chris stood up and walked to the front window with his back to Carrizo and Viggo. "You don't want to put your own people on this hunt and you damn sure don't want the Sheriff to call in the FBI or Texas Rangers. Is that about right?"

Carrizo smiled and stood up. Viggo held the man"s jacket open and he smoothly slipped back into it. "Your role here should be clear, Mr. Marcus."

Tru had had enough. "Why? Why involve us again? It was YOUR nephew who went off the reservation and tried his hand at kidnapping. It was YOUR nephew that stole your money. Fix this shit yourself. Everyone knows you have the manpower." Tru was angry and her face was hurting a bit.

Carrizo looked at her and the tic under his eye began a slow twitch. "Loose ends. I have no tolerance for loose ends Trudy. All of you are loose ends at this moment. To put it bluntly, you are absolutely correct. In 24 hours I can have all of this cleaned up. Yet I cannot bring myself to simply kill the four of you. It would be a waste. Viggo, of course, disagrees with me on this matter. I fear he feels I am becoming soft hearted." Viggo grunted softly in agreement, but said nothing. "Make no mistake, Trudy. It is not weakness. Think of it as sort of like playing chess with living pieces."

"Arrogant much?" Tru was livid and shouting now. "What guarantee do we have that when your game is over, we'll be left alone to live our lives? Or will you simply trash your current chess set and replace it with a new one?"

Chris had crossed the room and was standing behind his wife, ready to grab her if she lunged at Carrizo. The Sheriff was calm, but coiled like a spring. Anne was speechless in her chair. Viggo balanced on the balls of his feet and looked like he could possibly be in two places at once.

Carrizo though, was brushing imaginary lint off his lapel. He smiled coldly at the whole group and said "None of course. Your frustration is to be expected. As you say, the root of this fiasco is my nephew. He was the son of my wife's sister. Further direct involvement by me would only serve to increase the tension in my home. I can promise you that I have even less tolerance for discord in my bedroom than I have for loose ends."" Like a king, Carrizo turned on his heel and left the cabin without another word.

Viggo stopped at the door, reached in his coat pocket and laid an envelope on the entry table. Nodding at Chris, he said "You'll find the information you need here. The telephone number is my cellular. I will be available to assist you with supplies, cash or manpower." Everyone stood still and silent for several long minutes after they had gone. They listened to the Range Rover's engine start without moving. Once it faded into the distance, Chris stomped to the entry table and snatched the envelope up. The Sheriff lit a cigar without asking Tru's permission, something he would never have dreamed of doing ordinarily. Anne was pale and shaken, still seated. Tru went to her bedroom and dug an ancient pack of Virginia Slims out of her lingerie drawer.

"Smoking again, are we?" Chris asked when he saw her light up in the kitchen.

"Might as well. The Mexican Mafia will kill me long before the cigarettes at this rate." Tru shook a second one out of the pack and offered it to Chris. He declined, but said nothing else to her about it. Anne however, walked over and lit a cigarette herself.

The Sheriff stared in shock at his wife. "What the hell Anne?"

"Jonathon, honey, I've been a closet smoker for twenty years. Started when you got shot on that drug bust. There are worse things." Anne figured she might as well come clean. "For example being framed for bribery and losing everything you've worked so hard for." Anne sat down at the island next to Tru, using Carrizo"s coffee mug as an ashtray.

Chris and Ramos spread the contents of Viggo's manila envelope out on the coffee table. There was a Mexican passport for each of them , $2000 in cash, two photos of Hector on a boat with the name "Libertad" clearly visible, and a single printed page of information. Ramos held the Mexican passport in one hand and the cigar in the other hand. He glanced at Chris on his left and asked "How ugly do you think things would get if I just gutted Carrizo next time we see him?"

"Jonathon just call the Texas Rangers. Tell them everything. All of it out in the open and let the chips fall where they may." Anne lit a second cigarette and accepted the martini Tru had made for her.

"You know… I'm kind of leaning toward Jonathon and the whole gutting Carrizo." Tru was staring at Chris. He turned and met her eyes.

"Think that through a minute honey. We kill him and then what? Hector gets away scot free, the good Sheriff here is still screwed for bribery, and you and me? We're on the run forever from Carrizo"s cartel. Viggo will take it personally." Chris wasn't just stating the obvious, he knew his wife and the odds of her taking a pot shot at Carrizo the first chance she got were pretty good.

The sheriff chuckled and stood up, stretching his arms over his head as he walked to the front door. "Yeah… I really don't relish the idea of taking on Viggo. He won't ever let that sort of blemish to his professional record go unanswered."

Chris followed Ramos out to the porch, Tru and Anne stayed in the kitchen, drinking. Tru looked at Anne and said, "I don"t know about you, but I am NOT letting Chris do anything without me."

Anne nodded and sighed. "I'm not your girl for a fight. But I was a registered nurse and I have a feeling that"s a skill set we're going to need." She walked to Tru"s refrigerator and opened it. "Do you mind if I make us some burgers? I cook when I'm stressed."

The Sheriff and Chris sat in the rocking chairs on the porch looking over the paper and photos Viggo had left them. According to Carrizo's sources, Hector had sailed alone through the Gulf of Mexico and was spotted the day before off the coast of Campeche, Mexico. The photos had been taken from another boat some distance away, but there was no mistaking Hector's face. There was also a photo of his personal vehicle in a parking garage with the location and date written on it. "I did not know that. I knew he had used his E-Z Pass on one of the Houston toll roads, but not where he left the car." Ramos tapped the photo with one finger.

"This info sheet says he's off the coast of Campeche and that Carrizo's private plane will be available for our use. It's in Chihuahua city at a private air field. Jonathon, this puts us in direct contact with that man's business. Feels like quicksand." Chris was matter of fact. He knew they were already trapped, now it was just a matter of deciding how deep the sand was.

They sat around the table after Anne's burgers and baked potatoes had been consumed. Dinner had been quiet as they passed the photos and info sheet around the table. Tru grinned at Chris and asked, "You think there'll be time to take Carrizo's plane over to Mexico City?"

Chris laughed and pointed a finger at her across the table. "Shoes? You want to go to shoe shopping don't you?""

Tru smiled and batted her eyes at him. "The peso is weak and that means the shoes are cheap."

Anne and the Sheriff both laughed out loud. Chris was smiling, but his tone was serious. "Tru. You. Are. Not. Going. I won"t have you involved this time."

"You cannot be serious!" Tru slapped her

napkin down on the table. "I AM involved. Hello? Have you seen my face?" She turned to the side and put her cheek and blackened eye on full display.

"Your face is exactly why I don't want you down there. Jonathon and I can handle this. I want you at home. Not in Mexico, not in this cabin. AT. HOME." Chris sat back just a bit in his chair on the off chance his wife lost her temper for real and decided to fling a glass of tea in his face.

Tru actually fingered her tea glass for a moment before she walked out to the porch. Chris got up to follow her, but Anne stopped him. "You're wrong you know. The two of you", with a nod toward her own husband, "can find and kill Hector without our help. Leaving her behind is unfair. And probably unsafe. Who's to say Carrizo won't kill her while you're gone?"

Chris ground his teeth and followed his wife without a word. Anne and Jonathon began cleaning the kitchen without speaking either. They had been married for twenty eight years and the Sheriff knew he wouldn't win this fight any more than Chris would. After rinsing the dishes in the sink, Jonathon put his Stetson back on and escorted his wife to their truck. Chris was walking back from the barn without Tru. They said their good nights and Anne smiled at Chris. "We'll talk again tomorrow. Things will be clearer then."

Chris kissed Anne on the cheek and held her car door for her. "We'll see. 'Night Jonathon." When they had pulled out, he sighed and went back to the barn to try one last time to find a compromise with his wife. He really wanted Tru to go to their townhouse in New Orleans and wait this thing out. Hell, he would be happy if she went to her parent's place in East Texas or on a cruise down the Danube in Germany. It had always been Chris's intention to hunt Hector down, but on his own terms and in his own time. Being weaseled into doing it now by Carrizo and the Sheriff chapped his ass. Fighting with Tru about why she should let him handle this alone wasn't helping his mood and that didn't bode well for Hector when Chris eventually laid hands on him.

Chapter 31

Two Days Later

Chris and Tru were packing in the master bedroom at their farm in George West. They had brought all four of their horses home from the cabin and spent two days taking care of their business and getting caught up. Now they were putting a couple of days worth of gear in leather carry on bags for the trip to Mexico with the Ramoses. Two big hound dogs were sprawled out on their bed, two Doberman Pinschers were curled in arm chairs by the picture window and two more Rhodesian Ridgebacks were wallowing on plush dog beds in front of the fireplace. Chris had had the fireplace custom made for their bedroom - it was double the size of a normal unit and encased from floor to ceiling in round river rock. The warm climate meant the fireplace served most of the year as a location for the dogs to sit, lined up in a row for their nightly biscuit.

Chris watched his wife putting together her cosmetics travel bag and thought once more about just leaving without her. Facing her wrath when it was all over would cost him dearly. He figured a couple of expensive pieces of jewelry and a week or two sleeping in the guest room. The bonus payment would be a reduction in her faith in him and that was not a price he was willing to pay at all. Besides, Tru was a damn good shot with a pistol and he could trust her to cover his back no matter what. He reached down and zipped his bag closed, gently pushing a dog's nose out of the bag first. "Go pester your mommy, see what's in her bag." The Ridgeback gave him a pitiful look and rolled over on the bed with a disgusted grunt. Chris laughed and laid on the bed to wrestle with his dogs while Tru finished her packing.

 Tru watched Chris playing with the dogs and smiled too. All six of the big dogs were leaping around on the bed and floor with Chris, barking and laughter echoing off the tile floor. She tossed her make up bag in the carry on and sat in one of the arm chairs trying to wrestle a sneaker back from Gracie, one of the Dobermans. She had spent the morning riding three of her young horses just beginning their training and then a fast sauna. It was one of those really expensive luxuries that she did not know how they had lived without before they installed it. The sauna had relaxed her and helped her still sore muscles when they got home from West Texas. The thought crossed her mind that she might never leave Mexico this time, might never throw a ball for her dogs again or sit in that overpriced hotbox on a cold morning. Tru smiled at Chris and thought it would be worth any price if she could help get him in and out alive.

 They drove in silence to the Corpus Christi airport where a chartered private plane was waiting to take them to Chihuahua. Viggo had not been kidding when he said he would provide supplies and cash as needed. They could have flown commercial from San Antonio, but that would have involved half a day of travel just to get to the airport. They parked in the gated lot and were surprised when a uniformed steward greeted them and loaded everything on the back of a small, electric cart. A short ride later and they were dropped at the front of their plane. The pilot greeted them personally and offered glasses of champagne as they climbed the steps and entered the cabin. He passed a sealed, champagne colored envelope to Chris before returning to the flight deck.

Chris remained standing and opened the note while Tru nosed around the passenger cabin, playing with the state of the art electronic entertainment system. "Another note from Carrizo. Says he's pleased to provide our transportation and he wishes us success in our "endeavor"." Chris tossed the note on the closest seat. "Like we're off to work on our tans in Cancun. I swear to God, I want break my boot off in his ass."

"I wonder how pleasant his manners would be then?" Tru muttered and curled up in a leather window seat, sipping her champagne and opening a recent Town & Country magazine.

Chris sat in the seat facing hers with a disgusted snort. Then he stared hard at her left hand. The plane's engines changed pitch and it started a slow roll to the runway. "Really, Tru? You wore your damn ring? AGAIN?"

Tru glanced down at her emerald engagement ring in horror and slapped her forehead with her other hand. "I didn't even think about it! When you brought it back from the jeweler, I just put it on like normal."

Chris had a wicked grin on his face when he said, ""Need some help while you practice swallowing?" He was openly leering at her now and she couldn't help but smile, even as she swatted him with her magazine.

Three hours later they disembarked onto a hot tarmac landing strip. A private airport with only two hangars and a small commercial brick office building bearing a sign that said "Carrizo Enterprises". A second plane was already being guided out of one of the hangars and a black armored Range Rover waited for them next to the hangar. The back door of the SUV opened, revealing a casually dressed Viggo, carrying a silver Halliburton briefcase.

"Sheriff Ramos is already here Mr. Marcus."" Viggo pointed to the office building and then nodded at Tru. "All of you will take the second plane to Merida in the Yucatan. Go to the Merida house on the coast and follow the directions included in this case. There is a boat for your use at the Progreso marina. Your quarry was spotted sailing south along the coastal waters this morning." Viggo handed the case to Chris without another word. He got back in the Range Rover and drove away.

The sheriff and Anne came out of the building as Viggo sped off. "Chris. Tru. I wish I could say it was good to see you folks." It was the first time either of them had ever seen Jonathon Ramos out of uniform. He wore jeans, boots, his white Stetson and a tucked

in polo style shirt. So did Chris.

"Apparently they called each other to decide what to wear." Anne remarked when she and Tru hugged hello. That was when Tru realized both men had the same dark green polo shirt and faded jeans on. They walked back to the office and Chris handed the briefcase to Sheriff Ramos.

"Do the honors Jonathon. We're here on your behalf." Chris wasn't being unkind, just stating the facts as he saw them.

Tru had picked up a drink coaster from a stack near a coffee pot. "What is it with this stupid iguana with his tail on fire?" She waved it in the general direction of the group behind her before pouring two cups of coffee and walking back to Chris' side. "And why is this one on a checkerboard background? Those napkins Carrizo leaves laying around everywhere are a plain white background."

"If you're illiterate in any jungle in the world, doing business with the cartels and you see that Fire Iguana symbol, you know you're dealing with Jorge Carrizo." The Sheriff stated almost idly. "I don't know what the checkerboard symbolizes though."

"I think it's probably a chess board." Anne was studying the coaster closely.

Chris cleared his throat impatiently and got everyone's attention. "The case?"

Ramos ducked his head and opened the silver case. Inside were glossy 8x10 photos from the last 24 hours of Hector on the Libertad, two cell phones, a set of car keys, two single keys with an address in Merida attached to it, another typed sheet of information and two Colt 1911 .45 caliber pistols sitting in foam cutouts. The Sheriff hefted one of the pistols and checked the chamber before he said "At least it's a model I'm familiar with." The info page listed the cell phone numbers, a location of their vehicle and directions to the house and a marina in Progresso. One key was for the house and the other was apparently to a boat. Anne looked at each one of them in the silence and said "Anyone mind if I do some fishing while we're out there?" It took a second for the group to realize she was kidding and they all laughed. Tru was grateful for Anne's presence right now. Chris could be downright scary and cold as ice when angered. Right now he was on a slow, simmering burn that would eventually boil over like a volcanic eruption and destroy anything or anyone in his way. Anne's sweet nature and gentle humor brought a measure of humanity back to their immediate collective conscience.

Within a half hour they were all seated on yet another of Jorge Carrizo's private jets and buckled in for take off. It would be a short flight to Merida and Chris was already asleep. He had that uncanny ability to close his eyes and sleep anywhere, anytime. Tru envied him, she had suffered with insomnia for years. Jonathon and Anne were quiet, reading the magazine or looking out the window. Tru rummaged through the plane's galley and put together a small bag of fresh fruit, packaged snacks and small bottles of water. She tucked it all into her overnight bag and shrugged at the Sheriff when he whispered, "whatcha' doin'?" with a grin.

"If we get stuck out at sea or in the jungle down there, I want snacks. You have NO idea how nasty Chris can get without a daily dose of chocolate." The Sheriff and Anne both stifled chuckles, trying not to wake Chris.

"I resemble that remark." Chris opened one eye.

"It's like living with a vampire."" Tru said as she settled down into a window seat and watched the Gulf of Mexico glide by under the wing. The water was a dingy brown and grey along the Texas coast, the result of years of oil refineries and hundreds of drilling rigs and their associated pollution. But here, on the northern edge of the Yucatan Peninsula, the water was shades of deep green and inviting blues, dotted with sail boats and coral reefs.

"Say Sheriff, if you're down here chasing after your only deputy, who's at home minding the store?"" Chris yawned and stretched.

"I called in Bill Reynolds. You remember him, don't you? He was my deputy before Hector. Retired a couple of years ago, but he's still on the reserves list."

"Oh yeah. Bill's a good guy."" Chris reached into Tru's bag of goodies and pulled out a candy bar. "How much does he know about this circus?"

"I told him I needed a few days to take care of some personal business and Hector had resigned suddenly. Bill just shrugged and said he wouldn't mind picking up some hours for a few months. I think he's putting a new roof on his house, needs the money." The Sheriff accepted half the chocolate bar Chris was holding out to him.

Chapter 32

The city and Mexican state of Campeche was essentially a colonial era swamp, but the further into the Yucatan you went, the drier it became. It was still a humid jungle, but one without any surface water. No rivers, no streams and no lakes. The water was below the ground in deep limestone sinkholes called cenotes. The cenotes were considered magical by early Mayans and they appeared throughout the region with complexes of caves connecting many of them underground. The rule of thumb was if there were Mayan ruins, a cenote would be close by. Tru and Chris had spent a fair amount of time over the years hiking the Yucatan and exploring the ruins. They had an old friend with a lime orchard two hours south of the northern city of Merida. A social call didn't seem likely this trip.

The jet landed at a small commercial airport just outside of Merida. They had a short walk to their car, which turned out to be a Land Rover Defender. Chris ran his hand over the hood appreciatively and said, "Carrizo does have excellent taste. Wonder if he buys these things in bulk for a discount?"

"What? Like toilet paper at Sam's Club?" Tru grinned at him as she climbed into the back seat with Anne. Ramos took the passenger seat, leaving it to Chris to drive. Jonathon wasn"t fussy, he hated driving in Mexico. Merida was a huge city with outrageous traffic ranging from giant tourist buses to pickup trucks so overloaded with produce they were dragging the back fenders on the street. Turn a corner and you might actually end up at a red light behind a horse and cart.

Merida was a contrast of sorts. Not a tourist mecca like Cancun to the south, but not the metropolis of Mexico City. There was crime, of course, but as a rule Merida was mostly quiet and viewed as a summer home getaway for Mexico's wealthy elite. The American and European tourists tended to flock to the beaches of Cancun and Puerto Vallarta, leaving the beaches and coastal villages near Merida relatively unspoiled.

The group's destination was in a village southwest of the city. Celestun was a sleepy fishing village with a small marina and not much else. Carrizo's house technically had a Merida address, but it was located on the coast. The place was actually a small compound that Carrizo maintained strictly as a vacation home. The entire area belonged to another cartel, meaning Jorge Carrizo's flaming iguana did not do business in the Yucatan. He was known, of course, respected and shown certain courtesies, but he did not trespass financially. Viggo had already made contact with the local power base and had been assured that Chris and the Sheriff would be allowed to complete their mission without interference.

Tru read the directions to Chris as he weaved, honked, slammed on the brakes and cursed his way through the center of the city to the only highway leading to Celestun. Anne sucked in air and tried not to shriek when they slid to a sudden stop to avoid being run down by a city bus blowing through a red light. She tightened her seatbelt and decided not to look out the window again. Chris swerved suddenly to the right and slid to a stop against the curb in front of a coffee shop. He growled something incomprehensible to the other three, got out of the truck and stalked inside. Five minutes later he returned with cups of coffee for everyone and a pastry slathered in chocolate for himself. The Sheriff tucked his chin to his chest and tried to keep his laughing as quiet as possible.

An hour later they parked at the beach in Celestun and exited the truck. Chris and the Sheriff walked down to the marina to take inventory of the boats in dock on the off chance the Libertad happened to be in port. She wasn't. Anne and Tru wandered through the farmer's market, using some of Carrizo's cash to buy fresh produce and ten pounds of just caught shrimp. Dinner in hand, they drove on to the house outside of town proper. It sat on five acres, completely surrounded by a fifteen foot stone wall with glass shards protruding from every inch of the top. Three stories of modern glass and steel construction stared at them from the gated entry. There was one person manning the gate, openly carrying a MP5 9mm sub-machine gun when they approached. He took one look at each of them, matched their photos to their physical faces, then opened the gate without a word.

Once inside the house, Anne got to work shelling shrimp, making a lime and cilantro marinade and starting a pot of boiled potatoes and corn. Jonathon and Chris prowled the grounds and perimeter fence looking for weak spots. Tru took the elevator to the third floor and stood in awe at the 360 degree view. The entire third floor was floor to ceiling glass, nothing obstructed the view of the ocean and a mile of empty, white sand beach. There was a balcony with hammocks overlooking the pool and ocean below. The third floor was really just a surveillance tower in a pretty setting. As Tru completed her exploration of the house, she noted three safe rooms complete with fire and bullet proof doors and walls and self contained electronics, water and air supplies. There was a huge built in gun safe that looked like a closet at first glance. One of the three keys on the household key ring opened the heavy steel door. "This is the house I want to be in when the zombie apocalypse comes," she thought as she moved their luggage to one of the four master suites.

They ate dinner on the patio near the swimming pool. Skewered grilled shrimp and ice cold Tecate beer from the house supply. The Sheriff lit an actual Cuban cigar with a sigh of intense pleasure, again from the house humidor. Chris pointed at the cigar and said, "Have you just thrown your badge away now?"

"Son, I have dragged my wife with me to a man hunt in the Mexican jungle that will most likely end in the two of us digging a grave out there. Smoking a communist cigar taken from a drug lord seems like the least of my ethical worries tonight." Chris laughed heartily and reached for the second cigar himself.

Tru spread the contents of the briefcase out on the table and once again they passed the items around between them and discussed strategies. By the time they said goodnight, it was decided that Jonathon and Chris would take Carrizo's boat out in the morning, Tru would go with them, but stay with the vehicle on land and Anne would hold the fort at the house. She had no interest at all in dealing with Hector directly and she wasn't equipped emotionally to handle a possible shoot out. Her plan was to be ready to render first aid to whomever might need it.

The next morning arrived with dark clouds and wind. The gate guard was wearing a poncho and rain hat when Tru, Jonathon and Chris drove through. The Progreso port was almost two hours away from the house, but Progreso opened to the Caribbean sea, whereas Celestun faced the Gulf of Mexico. They wanted to try to catch Hector out on the water, but before he hit the actual ocean and vanished. Sailing back toward Celestun might provide them with the perfect opportunity and the least complications.

Chapter 33

Hector took his time once he left US waters. He was enjoying his freedom and learning the ins and outs of the Libertad. He had kept the coastline in view along the way, not entirely trusting himself just yet out in the open water. The boat was slicing the water smoothly and easily, the equipment was all in excellent working order and he was feeling pretty good. He considered docking in Campeche, but the marinas were crowded and there was no compelling reason to go to Campeche as opposed to Merida or Cancun. All three cities would have banks and ATM machines to access the remaining money in Houston. Twice he thought he had seen a cigarette boat following him, but he couldn't be sure and since they didn't stop or contact him, he pushed the sightings out of his mind. His police training suggested the cigarette boat was just normal drug runners taking care of their business.

He had been on the move for eight days now with no obvious pursuit. Hector felt confident the Sheriff had found his car by now and would be discovering the paper trail shortly. It was time to start moving his money around. He knew he should have done it earlier, but the truth was, he had been scared to go ashore in Northern Mexico. Hector wanted to be completely out of Carrizo's territory first.

He was probably an hour from the port of Progreso when the storm clouds began to build above him. The air turned heavy and the winds were kicking up white caps all around his boat. Hector fancied himself a world sailor, but he was in no way ready to handle a storm alone. He turned on the boat"s engine and cruised into Progreso. He could take a cab into Merida, handle his financial transfers, and replenish his food stores. Before leaving his boat, Hector put a small handgun in a shoulder holster and tugged a windbreaker on, covering the weapon nicely. He stopped at the marina office and paid for two days space rental in cash, then hailed a cab.

Hector's cab had just pulled onto the loop around Merida when Chris parked the Defender at the Progreso marina. He and the Sheriff reached under their seats and pulled out two sawed off 12 gauge shotguns. Both were Remington weapons with folding stocks. Two boxes of ammo were in the center console. They checked the weapons and put them back, carrying a shotgun of any size out onto a public street was not the sort of attention either man cared to draw. Both men carried the Colt 1911 pistols Viggo had given them in Chihuahua and Tru had chosen another Glock like her own from the house safe. When they had left the truck, she moved to the driver's seat and kept an eye out on the passersby for any sign of trouble.

Jonathon spoke briefly to the man in the marina office and returned to Chris' side, pointing toward the second dock. They walked carefully, but with purpose toward a sail boat at the end of the dock. It was empty and silent when they boarded it. Neither man spoke as they searched the deck. Convinced no one was hiding in a storage bin, they convened on the narrow door leading to the cabin below. Thunder boomed overhead as the sheriff slammed into the door with all his weight. It shuddered, but the lock did not give way. Chris went to a storage locker at the stern and dug around until he came up with a huge metal wrench. He kept an eye out for witnesses as Jonathon slammed the door three times before the wood splintered and swung inward a foot. The cabin below was dark and empty.

"Do we sit here and wait for him to return?" Jonathon looked at Chris in the dim galley.

"Where do you think he's gone?"" Chris asked.

"The market? Supplies maybe." Jonathon was digging around in the galley cabinets where canned goods were stacked neatly and secured with bungee cords. "Hell, he could have gone sightseeing for all we know."

"I vote we sabotage this damn thing. We wait for him to return and snatch him up. If we miss him somehow, he won't be going far. Then we take a look around town....see if we can spot him."" Chris was bouncing the wrench in both hands.

The sheriff nodded and they opened the trap door in the floor that led down to the engine room. Once there, Jonathon pulled the oil plug and let it stream out on the floor. Chris took the wrench and knocked a pair of nasty dents in the engine casing and broke open a storage bin. It held some basic hand tools, quarts of oil and a gym size blue duffle bag. Chris picked up a screwdriver in the bin and used it to puncture the fuel line, adding a steady drip of diesel to the puddle of oil underfoot. When the damage was done, Jonathon hefted the duffle bag and they went back to the deck, pulling the cabin door closed behind them. They walked down the dock as if they owned it, the duffle bag swinging from the Sheriff's hand.

Chapter 34

"Viggo. Tell me how our friends are doing."" Carrizo was knotting his tie in front of the massive mirror in his private closet. He was dressing for Miguel's memorial service. Viggo had been sent to the Yucatan to personally oversee the hunt and provide support as needed.

"Sir they have located the Libertad in Progreso. Hector is not with the boat. And it appears that they have taken a bag off the boat." Viggo was sitting in a truck half a block away from the still parked Defender.

"Good. That will be my cash. I assume you have the materials you will need?" Carrizo slid his feet into a pair of lizard loafers with tiny tassels.

"Just as you requested. I will make the installation when Mr. Marcus and Mr. Ramos have vacated the premises. Has the Houston bank been accessed yet?"

Carrizo slid into his suit coat and sighed deeply. "All of the funds were wired to two different accounts earlier today. Apparently, Hector has separated the original sum from the incentive amount I added. Does that seem strange to you, Viggo?"

Viggo paused, thinking about it. "Sir, Hector has shown himself willing to steal from you once already. Why would he separate the money? Why not just keep all of it?"

Carrizo froze mid stride as he exited his closet. ""Viggo…we have a new player in our game."

Hector stood at the Scotiabank counter in central Merida with a look of disbelief on his face. His voice was a mere croak when he asked the clerk to repeat what she had just told him.

"Senor, the account number you have given me shows only a balance of $23.64 American. Perhaps you do not have the correct numbers? Or lack the authority to make this transaction." she was haughty now. What sort of man comes to a bank and asks to wire transfer $23.64?

"That must be wrong. I have $100,000 in that account and I want to move it down here to THIS bank. Please check again."" Hector was sweating now and his face had turned pale.

For the third time the clerk sent the information request to Houston International Bank and for the third time the balance reflected was $23.64. This time she turned the computer screen toward Hector so that he could see it for himself. "If you have nothing else, senor, please step out of the line so that I may assist other customers."

Hector acquiesced and stood outside the building, hands shaking, knees weak and sweat beading on his brow. He was sick to his stomach when he got back in the cab. By the time he was half way to Progreso and his boat, the fear had begun to turn to anger. That was his money. HIS. Where was it? What had happened? More importantly, who had his money?

Chapter 35

Viggo watched the Sheriff and Chris get back into the Defender and toss the duffle bag in the second row seats. They sat there for thirty minutes before starting the truck and driving away. Viggo followed some distance. Once he realized that they were heading completely away from the marina, he drove back and strolled to the Libertad carrying his own duffle bag. He smirked at the broken lock on the cabin door, muttering "Amateurs." before entering himself. A professional would have had a lock picking kit on his person.

Viggo laid everything from his bag out on the tiny galley table before him. Satisfied that all the parts were accounted for, he sat down and began to build his bomb. The smell of diesel fuel wafted up from the engine room and Viggo tipped his head in the general direction of the dock. "Maybe less amateurs and a little more professional after all." A fuel spill that ignited would certainly be plausible with a first time solo sailor. None the less, Viggo attached his bomb to the back of the engine room door, keying the detonator to his cell phone. He smiled at his handy work, gathered up his tools and returned to his truck.

When the cab drew near the marina, Hector was wound up like a ten day watch. His newly acquired hyper paranoia kicked in and he told the driver to make a full pass down the street, past the marina and to drop him at the market instead. Out of the cab, Hector blended into the tourist crowd and watched just as Viggo exited the Libertad. He stopped breathing momentarily. Viggo was Carrizo's bodyguard and enforcer. If he was here, then

God only knew who or what else might be waiting for him. Hector darted into the first restaurant he came to and locked himself in a bathroom stall. He searched his wallet and pockets, finding $2500 dollars from the $72,000 in the duffle bag and little else. He sat heavily on the toilet and tried to figure out what to do.

Anne was ensconced in a lush chair in the office of Carrizo's vacation home. She plugged her laptop in. She had brought it with her for one specific reason. It was the only machine with the banking information stored on it and she had one last transaction to complete before Tru, Chris and her husband returned. She had been married to Jonathon for twenty-eight years. She wasn't sure what he would do about it, but she knew what he would not do. The Sheriff would never touch the money, much less keep a dime that Hector had been paid by the cartel. Anne understood his feelings, but she felt differently. She had no intention of letting Hector or Carrizo have the money back, even if her husband refused to use it. Once the internet connection was made, she logged into the Swiss account. It had been surprisingly easy to open the foreign accounts, she had the minimum amount required and all of Jonathon's identification information. It was simply a matter of waiting twenty four hours and paying the $75 fee to wire the money from Houston to the new banks.

Anne spent twenty minutes selecting and confirming her choices. She made electronic contributions of $5000 each to the Shriner"s Children's Hospital, the ASPCA, the US Humane Society, the Red Cross, Doctors Without Borders and Shelter Box. Each one received the money in the name of "Jorge Carrizo". $30,000 in cash gone forever in mere minutes. Anne laughed out loud as she clicked the enter button for the last time. She had no intention of touching a penny of the "incentive" $50,000 Carrizo had added to ensure Jonathon's participation in his game and later silence. That money belonged to the cartel and the strings attached were made of barbed wire. She grinned at the computer, looked up at a photo of Carrizo and his family on the wall and said out loud, "HA! Living chess pieces my ass. Betcha' didn't see THAT move coming." $70,000 remained in the Swiss account and Anne had yet to decide what to do with it. Technically, the money belonged to Jonathon Ramos and by law, as his legal wife, half of it belonged to her. She still had $20,000 to play with.

    Chris pulled the Defender into a dirt alley a block back from the water and parked alongside a wall surrounding another antique beach house. They sat in silence for a moment before Tru asked, "What now? You got Carrizo's money back. Let's just go. Or do we sit here and wait for Hector to come back?"

    "Pretty much. We'll spread out to spots where we can watch the marina and wait." Chris pocketed the truck keys and they piled out into the alley. "I still have a personal issue to discuss with our boy."

    Chris walked into a pharmacy over looking the dock, Jonathon strolled over to the market and lurked among the vegetable stalls, and Tru took a seat at an outdoor table of a tiny taco shack. She had just ordered a plate of fried shrimp when Hector let himself out of the toilet stall and washed his face in the sink. The rain started, light, but irritating none the less. It forced Jonathon to move under the patio cover and take a table opposite of Tru"s. His back was to the restrooms inside the café, but Tru could see inside on her right and out to the marina on her left. Chris's vantage point allowed him to see the Libertad, the corner of the alley where they had parked and his wife, but not inside the restaurant. He stood in the window, the rain providing a convenient excuse for simply loitering in the pharmacy. They waited.

Viggo sat in his old beat up Nissan truck on the main street, the dock to his left, the pharmacy and taco shack ahead and on his right. He had the only clear view of all the players. He grinned when he saw how they had positioned themselves. He double checked the status of his cellular connection when the rain began. The bomb was merely a last ditch option on the off chance that the Sheriff and the Marcus couple screwed up and allowed Hector to escape. In the end, Senor Carrizo wanted Hector dead. His preference was to have these people handle it themselves, but his habit was to look ahead at all possible outcomes and prepare for each. Thus Viggo had followed them to the Yucatan and made sure that no matter what else happened, Hector Williams was finished. Viggo watched the Sheriff sip a cup of coffee and wondered who had taken the Houston money. He could not remember the last time someone outwitted or surprised his boss, had to have been years.

Suddenly, Viggo's eyes narrowed and he leaned forward over the steering wheel for a closer look. It was Hector. Peering through the front door of the taco place, staring at the Sheriff's back. Tru had spotted the man, but hadn't moved an inch. Viggo cut his eyes toward the pharmacy and saw Chris was staring at his wife, then at Hector in the doorway. Viggo's blood began to pump a little faster, he loved a good hunt and this one was beginning to shape up nicely. Part of him wanted to just put a bullet in Hector's head and get on with his business, but the boss wanted things to happen in a particular way. So Viggo stayed in his truck and watched. He wished he had some popcorn.

Chapter 36

Hector was frozen at the doorway. He would know Jonathon Ramos with his eyes closed and now he was staring at the man's ramrod straight back less than 40 feet away. He groaned out loud when he realized Tru Marcus was sitting at a second table as well. "Shit." He looked at the dock and it was empty in the rain, but he knew there was no way he could make it to the Libertad and set sail. The Sheriff would physically be on him before he untied the first set of knots. Though he was more worried about the Marcus woman just shooting him as he ran by; women were screwy that way.

Hector caught a movement out of the corner of his eye and jerked to the left just in time to see Chris Marcus walking out of the pharmacy next door. He knew the Libertad was definitely out of his reach now. The Sheriff turned and began surveying the area intently when he realized Chris was moving his direction and Hector backed away from the door, into the shadows. He turned and darted through the restaurant and into the kitchen area, pushing a waiter to the side as he passed. In the kitchen, he shoved his way past line cooks, waiters and busboys, moving fast to the back door. The door was propped open with a case of glass bottle Cokes. Hector kicked the case away from the door, slamming it behind him and then propped the Cokes against the door from the outside. Effectively blocking the door at least for a few moments. He ran down the alley, feet pounding and churning the mud as the rain seeped under his shirt collar and splattered off his windbreaker. Skidding around the first corner on the right, he saw a motorcyclist just pulling away from the curb. Hector rushed the rider from the side and pushed him and the bike off balance. As the man tried to right himself and stop his bike from toppling onto his leg, Hector jerked the handle bars toward him. The rider tipped backward and Hector shoved him the rest of the way off. It had been years since he had ridden a motorcycle, but it came back to him fast enough. As he revved the engine and shot into the road, he could hear shouting behind him. Hector made a direct run to Highway 261 toward Merida, the only thought in his head was to weave through the jungle and try make his way back to the coast further south of Progreso. From there he would use his cash to pay a fisherman to deliver him to the Libertad in the night. Maybe he could get aboard from the water and be gone before they realized he was even there.

Chris saw Hector whirl around in the restaurant behind the Sheriff and sprinted forward. Tru stood up and ran to the doorway at the same time, Jonathon was steps behind her. Viggo cursed and started his truck, jumping into traffic without looking and speeding down the block. Horns blared in his wake. Tru made it inside first and pushed the poor waiter down for the second time, elbowing her way into the kitchen where the cooks were still staring wide eyed at their kitchen door. Sheriff Ramos and Tru hit the door at the same time, it slammed open and bounced back against the exterior wall, scattering the case of glass bottles to the ground. Tru slipped on the broken glass and fell to the ground, her ankle twisted painfully beneath her. Chris was moving so fast, he had to jump over her legs to avoid trampling her in his rush.

"GO, just GO. I'll be fine." She shouted as both men slowed and began to turn to help her. Tru pulled herself back to her feet, using the door handle for leverage. She hobbled at a painful trot down the muddy alley, getting soaked in the process, the rain falling harder now.

Chris and Jonathon shot around the corner just in time to see Hector snatching the motorcycle from the teenager and riding off. Jonathon hollered Hector's name at his back. The man didn't even look back. "COME ON, the truck! Let's get the truck, I'm not losing this son of bitch now." Chris was moving to the right at the next alley where they had left the Defender, the motorcycle racing up the street ahead of them.

They drove the Defender back to the main street just as Tru was coming out of the first alley behind the taco shack. She waved them on, cupping her hands over her mouth and shouting at Chris' rolled down window. "Go get him! I'll call a cab and meet you at the house later. GO GO GO GO!"

Chris nodded and sped away, mud flying up behind the tires as he left the dirt alley for the paved main road Hector had taken. The Sheriff looked back once at Tru as she leaned against a building wall, heaving with her left ankle held up slightly. Tru turned to limp back to the restaurant when a small white Nissan truck stopped in front of her and a familiar Russian accent called her name.

"Mrs. Marcus! Get in." Viggo leaned over and opened the passenger door for her. True eyeballed him for a moment and decided she had nothing to lose by hitching a ride with Viggo. Once she was inside with the door closed, Viggo took off on the same track as Chris, Jonathon and Hector.

"Should I even ask what you're doing down here?" Tru used her shirttail to wipe some of the rain water off her face while Viggo shifted gears, weaving between cars as he tried to make up the distance between them and Chris.

"My job to keep things running smoothly for Mr. Carrizo. You know this." Viggo glanced out of the corner of his eye at her. He had no intention of making a pass at her, but he was still a man and could not resist a peek at her exposed bra while she tried to dry off.

"Making sure we do the job. I can promise you that Chris will kill Hector. There's no way around it, this is personal." Tru was pulling her hair into a wet pony tail with the ever present scrunchy from her pocket.

"I agree. Smoothly is the issue here. Mr. Carrizo dislikes loose ends and I am here to ensure there are none at the end of the day." Viggo shifted gears calmly and the little truck swept past a delivery van. The Defender was one car length ahead of them, racing through the rain and they could barely see Hector's motorcycle further ahead. Thunder boomed overhead, drowning out the sounds of the engine. "Why did they leave you behind?"

"I fell and twisted my ankle. They did not 'leave' me behind, I told them to go on without me. Seemed like the most efficient option." Tru couldn't help grinning as she watched the massive Viggo trying to use the clutch without his knee banging into the steering wheel. "Why in the hell don't you have a truck that fits you? You look like a cat in a hamster wheel."

Viggo laughed before he could stop himself. "I was blending."

Tru shook her head and said, "Blending? Honey, I don't know how to break it to you, but you're too big to blend any where."

Viggo grunted and whipped the little truck around a pickup so overloaded with cucumbers and melons it was tilting to one side. ""But I can tiptoe and dance like Baryshnikov when I want to. Where is this fool going?"

The motorcycle slid into the round about as the road merged with the loop around Merida proper. Hector gunned the bike across three lanes of traffic and was sling shot out of the circle onto the loop. Chris had to slow down, the Defender was top heavy, moving through an angle at high speed was a recipe for a roll over. Viggo blocked a big truck behind them, allowing Chris to maneuver across the three lanes with no further interference. Tru closed her eyes and prayed Viggo's plan wasn't to cause a diversion via a ten car pile up.

Hector revved the motorcycle to the redline once he was out of the round about. He shot down the loop and realized there was no easy way to turn back toward the ocean. The only real highway was the one into Progreso; he would have to head further south before there was another direct road to the coast. Maybe he could lose his pursuers on the back roads in the jungle and then just go directly back to the Libertad. He only needed a ten minute head start once he reached the docks. Ahead he noticed a road sign for Uxmal Archeological site. Hector merged into the lane exiting the loop for Highway 261 South and pulled further ahead of the Land Rover Defender carrying Chris and Jonathon.

Tru pointed for Viggo and said "Surely he"s not going into the jungles? There are so few roads out here, where does he think he's going to hide?"

Viggo grunted as he followed the Defender off the loop and onto 261 South. "Maybe he thinks he will lose us out there and double back. It's what I would do."

Tru stared at the rain and traffic ahead of them for a long time before she replied. "Viggo, let me ask you something. Why are we here? You are perfectly suited for this work. It would have been considerably less expensive and faster for Carrizo to just send you after Hector instead of all of us."

Viggo snarled at the truck as he ground the gears trying to get his big foot off the clutch. He was perched forward trying to see through the driving rain. "Mr. Carrizo is a wealthy man. He has traveled the world, produced an heir, doubled the size of his territory." He put the truck behind the Defender and the traffic began to ease as they got further from the city. "He has the ear of politicians in several countries. He's bored. His world is controlled, structured and he likes it that way, but he is always seeking entertainment."

Tru shook her head in disgust. "I just wanted to take my friend's two children on a trail ride. That's all. Now I'm a Goddamn pawn in a bored psycho's chess game." She pointed at Viggo, yelling now, "You realize that this was NOT what I asked Santa for. A concussion, fractured cheek, twisted ankle…. NOT MY IDEA OF ENTERTAINMENT!"

"I forget the last time a woman screamed at me and lived." Viggo's tone was mild, but Tru suddenly remembered who Viggo was.

Chris and Jonathon were gaining on the motorcycle. Jonathon was loading the shotguns with shells while Chris drove. When Hector led them off the loop and onto the highway leading to the interior of the Yucatan, Chris' eyes lit up. "Jonathon I think we can run him off the road up here. This highway drops to two lanes pretty quick and there will be a town that he can't avoid coming up. Tixul or Ticul or something like that. My buddy has a lime farm about an hour from here."

The Sheriff began digging in the glove box for a map and replied, "Seriously? You know this area?"

"Yep." Chris angled the Defender around a car straining to tow an ugly old station wagon behind it with a rope that was unraveling with every mile. "Been down this highway a few times over the years. What I don't know is if Hector knows where he's going or not."

The Sheriff was staring intently in the side mirror and then turned around in his seat and stared hard through the back window at the little white truck on their tail. "Well, what do you know? That's our boy, Viggo back there and I think he has Tru with him."

Chris looked into the rearview mirror with a sigh. "Damn. I wanted Tru out of this. It just figures she would hitch a ride with Carrizo's land shark."

Jonathon chuckled and said, "Son, you haven't been married long enough, but one day you'll admit that you don't understand that woman. I know my Anne looks docile to outsiders, but she's probably poisoned every spice bottle in Carrizo's house by now and stopped up the plumbing with Quickcrete and paint varnish."

Chris stared at the Sheriff for a moment trying to see if he was kidding or not. "Remind me to be nicer to Anne in the future." Jonathon nodded and began studying the map as the miles swept by, Hector in view ahead and Viggo's truck right on their bumper.

"Ok, there is a four way stop a few miles ahead. If Hector slows or stops there, we can ram him on the road. Otherwise, we"ll be in another populated area when we get to Ticul Municipality. The next town is Oxkutzcab, looks small." They watched in astonishment as the four way intersection appeared and Hector blew through it without slowing down. A big box truck slammed on its brakes, hydroplaning on the wet road and narrowly missing Hector's bike. The cab of the truck swung to the left and Chris was forced to jerk to a sideways stop across both lanes. Chris watched the truck swerve and regain control ahead of them while Jonathon watched Viggo behind them gearing down and heading for the ditch to the right. Within seconds, the box truck was straight and out of the center of the intersection. Chris dug into the Defender's horsepower and full time four wheel drive, correcting his own jackknife and resuming the pursuit, cursing at the top of his lungs. Viggo spun the back wheel on the slippery mud lining the ditch, but the other three tires caught on the pavement, propelling them back into the lane.

Hector bent over the handle bars of the bike and gunned it away from the intersection. He could hear the skidding and squealing of tires behind him, but he didn't dare look. He was trying to put some distance between himself and the Sheriff, trying to find a road to turn off on that would lead him back toward the ocean instead of further into the ancient Mayan jungle. He saw a sign pointing left with a picture of a pyramid on it - 12 kilometers away. Left was the general direction back toward the ocean and it beat the hell out of continuing straight. Hector slowed and made the turn, the rain sweeping against his face, half blinding him.

Chris could barely see the bike ahead of them and then in a flash it was gone. He slammed his hand against the dashboard and turned on the Defender's roof lights. Jonathan hollered out and pointed to the left "There! Single tail light on the left ahead, turning." Chris nodded and started to slow down for the turn.

"Where's my wife?"

"Right behind us." Jonathon looked over his back shoulder and saw the white Nissan truck mere feet off their bumper.

"Any chance we have that cell number for Viggo?" Chris floored the Land Rover's big V-8 engine as he came out of the turn.

"Got it saved on my phone. What do you want to tell him?" The sheriff pulled out the burner phone Viggo had given them in Chihuahua the day before.

"Tell him to dump my wife off in the next town or tourist spot. And ask him what sort of arsenal he's packing back there." Jonathan nodded and dialed Viggo's phone.

Viggo answered via his Bluetooth earpiece. He listened for a moment as he too negotiated the turn onto the ruins road. "Nyet. I cannot do that Mr. Ramos. Of course I have additional weaponry if you require it." He disconnected the call with a glance in Tru's direction. "Your husband would prefer I leave you at the next village."

"Is that what he said?" Tru turned in her seat to face Viggo, rubbing her sore ankle with one hand. "You would think he's never met me. He knows better than that."

"I believe his vish is for you to remain out of harm's way. Or maybe he thinks I vill use you as a hostage if he fails to dispose of Hector." Viggo looked away from the road for a moment and directly at Tru. "Perhaps you are too veak now to go on. Injured again."

"Veak? Why is your accent so heavy all the sudden?" Viggo's clear voice normally held only a hint of his Russian accent. Now though, it was so strong certain words were coming out deformed.

Viggo sighed and rubbed his face with one large paw of a hand, the other gripping the steering wheel like a vise. "When I am aggravated, the Mother Tongue wants out." This time his voice was crisp and clean. A determined effort.

"You're aggravated? Shut up. All you have to do here is drive, watch and report back to your boss." Tru"s tone was disgusted.

"No vonder he vants you some vhere else. You drivink me crazy!" Viggo slammed the truck down a gear to make a sharp curve without running over the top of Chris and the Sheriff.

Tru laughed with genuine humor. "Look here Colonel Klink, that just means you're getting to know me.

Viggo said nothing for a long time, just drove with his lips moving as he muttered to himself so softly that Tru couldn't hear him at all. When he finally spoke to her again, it was to ask if she was armed.

"Yes." Tru pulled the Glock out of the holster in her waistband at the small of her back. Viggo nodded approvingly.

"Glock is a good weapon. It's what I carry."

"See there? We do have something in common. You'll like me yet Viggo, just wait and see." Tru replaced her gun in the holster. Viggo snorted.

"HEY! Viggo! I know where we are. A couple of miles ahead is a Mayan ruin that's being excavated for the first time. This highway goes right past it. There should be a road to the right up here that cuts around the ruins and picks up this road again on the other side. If you can wring any more speed out of this truck, we might be able to cut Hector off."" Tru was searching the side of the road for the cutoff.

Viggo thought a moment and decided it wasn't the worst idea. Just then the Land Rover began to slow and Tru shouted "THERE! Turn now, it's that gravel road here." Viggo made the turn as the Land Rover ahead sped up again.

Hector could hear the Defender's big engine roaring behind him, but it wasn't visible in his rearview mirror. The wind was picking up and the rain was still blowing in his face, without a helmet he was having difficulty seeing the road ahead. When the engine of his bike sputtered, it took three tries for him to be able to see the fuel gauge. The indicator hovered just below the empty mark. Hector couldn't believe it. It had not even occurred to him to check the gas tank when he was stealing the bike in the first place. He felt a cold chill run down his spine and knew he was in trouble. There was no way he was going to let Sheriff Ramos drag him back to Texas and prison.

He saw the entrance to the ruins ahead on the right and swerved through the gate as the engine sputtered again and he began to lose speed. He rode past the unmanned gate and an empty portable building covered in signs with pictures of men in hardhats and red exclamation marks. He guided the bike behind the first lump of rock he came to and jumped off. The bike flopped on it's side and the engine finally died. Hector turned in a frantic circle and took off running on a narrow dirt path through the bushes. He had one hand on the butt of his pistol while he ran. There was a half exposed temple dead ahead with steep steps leading up. At the base was a set of hand carved steps leading beneath the temple. They were lined with dig tools and cordoned off from the public that normally traipsed about in nicer weather. Hector ducked under the rope and shot down the steps two at a time, water sluicing down the sides as he ran.

Chapter 37

Anne was lounging in a deep chair on the patio watching the rain fall with a cup of chai tea in her hand. She was still trying to decide what to do with the remaining money when the house phone rang. Startled, Anne bounced out of the chair and clutched her heart for a moment. "Get a grip girl." she whispered to herself and went to answer the phone.

"Hello?" Anne's tone was hesitant, it wasn't her phone and she doubted telemarketers would be calling the Carrizo family.

"Mrs. Ramos. Good afternoon." It was Jorge Carrizo. Anne took a deep breath before she replied.

"Senor Carrizo, what can I do for you?""

Carrizo was in his study with his feet propped up on his giant antique desk. He loosened his tie and removed his cuff links while he spoke to Anne. "I am delighted that you answered my telephone. You are just the lady I most want to converse with."

Anne walked to the kitchen with the phone glued between her ear and her shoulder so she could use both hands to fix herself a drink. A stiff drink. "How can I help you?" She pulled a brandy snifter from the cabinet and a bottle of whiskey in a crystal decanter.

"I was hoping you would enlighten me as to where Hector Williams' ill gotten gains have gone." Carrizo was friendly, almost as if he were amused. He pulled a cigar from his desk top humidor and waited for her answer.

Anne took another deep breath and a sip of the straight whiskey to steady her nerves. "Why would you think I was the person to ask?" Buying time while she got her backbone properly aligned.

"Because dear lady, your donations, made in my name no less, traced back to my house ISP. It is a private, secure, satellite connection. Let me just say how much I appreciate the sentiment, I do already support Shelter Box and the ASPCA." Carrizo was staring a photo on his desk of his daughter in Japan immediately after the 2011 earthquake. She was standing with a group of other volunteers, all wearing green Shelter Box shirts and ready to begin building temporary housing.

Anne froze, she knew Carrizo would trace the donations and money back to her, she just didn't realize it would be within HOURS. "I'm sorry, but I was certain you said you had no interest in that money?"

"Perhaps. And what are your plans for the remaining funds?" he refocused his gaze to the window facing the back lawns and the helipad. The chopper was already warming up, it's rotors whirring, waiting to take him to the airstrip. It was time to see things for himself.

"Why do you assume I have anything to do with this money?" Anne wasn't being belligerent, she really wanted to know.

"Your husband is far too constrained. Mr. and Mrs. Marcus have no access to the account. Simple deduction points to you, Mrs. Ramos." Carrizo stood up and removed his tie. "I will be happy to continue this conversation in person. Perhaps you will dine with me?"

Anne almost choked on the whiskey. "I"ll cook you a chicken fried steak when we return home." It was all she could think of on the spur of the moment.

Carrizo gave a soft chuckle and said, "I rather think that would be too much for our esteemed Sheriff. No, I shall come to you. After all, what sort of host would I be if I left you on your own?" He broke the connection and strolled out of his study, down the great hall and onto the back lawn. Within moments he was in his chopper and heading for the air strip.

Chris slowed when he realized the water was pooling on the roadway and he had lost sight of the motorcycle. The Sheriff was looking for any sign of the bike as well. "STOP!" he said suddenly. Then he rolled down the passenger window and listened through the falling rain on the metal roof of the Land Rover. "He turned up here somewhere, I can hear the bike engine to the right. Sounds like it's missing or running out of gas." Jonathon and Chris grinned at each other - they had him now.

Another 200 feet and they turned into the ruins entrance. The gravel and mud road showed the bike's track immediately. Jonathon pulled both shotguns from the backseat and held them at the ready in his lap. Chris parked the Land Rover just behind the fallen motorcycle and turned the engine off. Obviously Hector was now on foot, but where? Jonathon handed a shotgun to Chris and they stepped out of the truck, using the open doors for cover just in case Hector was lying in wait behind a rock or in the trees. The rain was tapering off to a light drizzle, water running off in streams through the mud all around their feet. Jonathon was inspecting the ground around the bike, he waved Chris over and pointed at the footprints leading toward the ruins. The men pulled apart, shotguns at the ready, and followed the tracks through the mud.

Viggo slowed on the dirt road and pointed through the trees on his left. "You see that? Looked like a motorcycle darted through there. I think Hector is in the excavation site."

Tru leaned in his direction, trying to see through the rain and vine covered trees to the ruins. "If he's over there, then we ought to be as well." She pulled out her Glock, checked the magazine, and chambered a round before returning it to the holster behind her back.

Viggo glanced at her and thought about how easy it would be to underestimate this woman. She was flippant and silly, clearly clumsy as hell, but she handled her weapon comfortably and he had never seen her show fear. Besides she was the one who shot Miguel the first time. Assuming Tru Marcus was just a girl and not to be taken seriously might get you killed and Viggo sort of liked that about her. His boss had chosen his players well.

Viggo stopped the Nissan truck behind some over grown bushes and flowering hibiscus plants. The rain was finally relenting as the two of them exited the vehicle. Viggo opened the tool box in the truck bed and pulled out a machete and a shotgun of his own. He offered one to Tru and she shook her head, saying "I suck with the long guns. If you've got another magazine for my Glock, I'll take that." Viggo handed her a full magazine and she tucked it into the front pocket of her jeans alongside her Blackberry. "What else you got in that magic box?" she grinned at Viggo and leaned over the truck wall for a peek.

Viggo held out an arm to prevent her from getting too close and said "Consider it like your Santa's bag. Full of goodies, but none belong to you." She huffed at him and walked away to peek through the brush in time to see Chris and Jonathon approaching the temple. "Psst! Viggo!" she waved behind her back for him to come look.

Together they watched Chris and the Sheriff split up, Chris went up the temple steps and Jonathon went down to the fresh dig area. Being younger, Chris had a much easier time bounding up the side of the pyramid than Jonathon would have in his place. At the pinnacle of the temple, Chris could see the entire complex laid out before him. Two buildings had been fully uncovered, two others were in partial stages of discovery and there were freshly opened ditches and pits scattered everywhere. The archeologists had been working this site with a vengeance for some time. A short distance beyond the temple, Chris could see a lush limestone circle in the ground, water shimmering in it as the sun began to peek out from the clouds. A cenote hidden in the jungle, forgotten for who knew how many centuries. What Chris didn't see was any sign of Hector on the grounds which meant he had to have gone into the tunnel under the temple.

Viggo wanted to follow Chris, but Tru put her hand on his arm and said "Wait. There will be more than one exit down there. These temples were always connected to underground caves or tunnels and the cenotes."

"What is a cenote?" Viggo spent time in Mexico, but the Yucatan wasn't Carrizo Cartel territory, so he had no interest in the region's history. Tru explained it to him and Viggo was silent for a long minute. "Ok. We go to the water hole and we see what we see. If there is another entry, we use it. If not we come back and do things my way."

Tru darted through the ancient trees around the far side of the temple toward the cenote. There were tiny frogs on the water filled blooms of African Tulip plants as they reached the edge of the cenote. The limestone rim disguised a three foot drop to the actual water below. Ancient mahogany trees lined one side of the pool where the rock ledges ended, vines as thick as a man's leg entwined around and connecting the trees to each other. On the far side of the cenote ledge were depressions in the rock leading down to the water. Tru went directly to the depressions and began to descend into the water, her gun held in one hand above her head when she stood waist deep in the crystal clear water. Tiny fish swarmed around her legs beneath the surface. Viggo paused at the ledge and watched her closely. Tru was searching for something along the outer edges of the rock, using her free hand to feel around under the water. "HERE! Viggo, it's here."

Tru found the opening to an underwater tunnel with her free hand. She said a prayer that the Glock could withstand a brief submerging. Her Blackberry was always in an Otterbox case and should be water proof. Tru sucked in a huge breath before she ducked under the surface and pushed her way into the tunnel. She swam for about a minute before an air pocket opened above her head. She was able to stand in the hollow, her head and shoulders completely out of the water. The tunnel continued and curved back toward the temple ahead of her. She ducked back into the water and popped out near Viggo's feet, surprising him enough that he jumped back as if she were a snake. "Come on big man. It'll be a tight squeeze for you, but the tunnel leads back toward the temple behind us." And then she was gone.

Viggo frowned and snarled, "I hate women,"" before he followed her into the water and the narrow tunnel. He popped up like a bubble at the air pocket. Tru made a concentrated effort not to laugh when she saw him. Disheveled, hair laying willy nilly on his head, the machete in his left hand and his short shotgun in the right. The look of utter disgust on his face reminded Tru of a pissed off Persian cat.

"Remind me to wring your neck later,"" was all he said to her when he was able to draw enough breath to speak. Tru said nothing, just led the way from the pool to the tunnel entrance, Viggo had to duck his head to avoid catching it on the low stone ceiling.

Hector hit the bottom of the steps and had to make a choice. The path split with a turn to the right under the temple itself and straight to God knows where. There were no lights down here, just some scattered glow sticks here and there, the poor grad student's version of emergency lighting. A pile of wooden crates full of straw and bubble wrap were stacked against the wall and a small personal flashlight on top of the stack. Hector snatched the light up and shot to the right, under the temple. The air smelled dry and damp at the same time. The walls were lined with carved limestone and holes at regular intervals where torches could be placed for illumination. The tunnel stopped in what looked like a dead end at first glance. When Hector shone his light on the wall in front of him he realized there were two recessed doorways with no doors. One had steps leading up to the interior of the pyramid temple and the second had stairs leading further down into the earth. A huge green iguana sat guarding the first doorway, watching Hector with one green eye, the tip of his tail flicking against the stone floor. Hector had a moment of irrational fear as the image of Carrizo's flaming iguana came to his mind's eye. He snarled at the iguana and ran past it, narrowly missing its head with his boot. Hector rounded a corner to the left and found himself in an alcove with a heavy stone table in the center and what appeared to be a drain of some sort carved into the floor from the table pedestal. Hieroglyphs were etched all along the base and the walls behind the table. He could hear footsteps echoing down the first hall he had traveled. He crouched down behind the pedestal, listening while he un-holstered his pistol. Then he waited in the dark for whomever was following him.

    Chris was far enough behind the Sheriff in the underground passageway that he couldn't see the man, but he could hear his boots ahead. Every step echoed off the stone walls and ceiling. He wanted to call out to Jonathon, but he also did not want to spook their prey if he was holed up further down the tunnels. Chris stopped at the chamber with the two recessed openings and listened. He heard a soft scraping noise to his left and began to move toward the steps leading further down. Chris had just ducked his head into the doorway when he heard three gunshots ahead. So loud and sudden he jerked back and to the side, whirling around with his back plastered against the wall. He gripped his shotgun in both hands, ready to fire. There were no additional shots fired and he could hear footsteps and a faint groaning beyond the doorway. Chris was sure he had heard a pistol and one report from a shotgun. He closed his eyes for a split second and took a deep, steadying breath before he ducked into the new hallway, keeping his back to the wall and moving sideways.

    Viggo and Tru had just crawled out of the water and were sitting on a dry spot on the floor of the tunnel that lead up and away from the cenote. They were under the temple now and it was pitch black. Viggo broke open his shotgun and poured water out of the barrel, he repeated the process for his Glock as well. Tru handed him her weapon and pulled out her Blackberry. It was fine, dry and in working order inside it's protective case and the flashlight application worked with the press of a button. She shined the light around the passage and held the beam on Viggo's hands while he unloaded each of their pistols, wiped them down as best he could and reloaded them. He handed hers back to her, butt first with a shrug that said it was the best he could do.

"Thanks. Still have your machete?" Tru holstered her weapon and shone the light around the floor at their feet.

"Certainly. This is not my first job."" Viggo flashed a feral smile at her and tilted his head toward the tunnel. ""Ready? Or do you need to paint your nails first?"

Tru punched him in the shoulder and stood up. ""I had no idea you had a sense of humor!" She led the way to the first turn in the tunnel where the ceiling was finally tall enough for Viggo to walk fully upright.

"You want to take point now that you don't have to lumber like a gorilla?"

Viggo shot her a look that would have been dangerous had there been enough light to see it by. He had just stepped alongside her when they heard the three shots in the distance. Viggo instantly reacted, pushing Tru back and against the wall with his left arm, the machete still held tightly. He leaned back next to her and whispered, "Take the blade."

Tru put her phone back in her pocket, grabbed the machete handle from him and tried to slow her heart rate down. Viggo brought the shotgun up, pumped it once and began to walk forward, slowly and meticulously. Tru was three steps behind him desperately afraid for Chris, but unable to offer him any assistance. The tunnel turned again and the grade increased as they got further away from the cenote and closer to the bowels of the temple. It was maybe seven foot tall and less than eight foot wide, the floor was a layer of dirt over more limestone. The walls were covered entirely in primitive, hand carved pictographs and hieroglyphs. Tru had a distinct sense of stepping back into history and feeling very much like an uninvited guest.

Chapter 38

A beep caused Jorge Carrizo to look at his smart phone. The GPS tracker had alerted and sent him a message. The Land Rover Defender"s tracking beacon had stopped moving and the vehicle was now still. Carrizo raised an eyebrow as the map came into focus showing the vehicle parked at a newly discovered ruin site about 40 miles south of Merida. A bemused expression crossed his face as he spoke to himself, "The middle of the jungle. Not near the ocean. It appears the pawns have become rooks."

He was sitting in the back of his signature Range Rover, the driver his only companion as they approached the Celestun beach house. Just before his plane had landed in Merida, he had called the housekeeper and asked her to meet him at the house to prepare dinner in three hours. He wanted some time to visit with Anne Ramos in private. Mrs. Ramos was turning out to be far more interesting that he had previously given her credit for. A look into her background explained part of it. Her history was sparse, but revealing. Orphaned at thirteen, in and out of seven foster homes before she was eighteen years old. She had gone to nursing school at Stephen F. Austin University in east Texas. She worked as a registered nurse for some years before and after marrying the now Sheriff Jonathon Ramos. They had two children, one who died in a car wreck before his 20th birthday and another son currently living in Chicago. Carrizo had the distinct feeling that Anne was a far better chess player than he had given her credit for. He was looking forward to spending some time with her.

  Anne stood in the third floor tower watching the road as the Range Rover passed through the gate. She had taken the intervening hours since her conversation with Carrizo to move the last $20,000. She purchased bearer bonds from a variety of different sources. $5000 each for both of the Burgess twins and the remaining $10,000 for her own son. The orders had been placed, paid and were in the process of being shipped to the boys. The remaining $50,000 in Jonathon's name was still sitting the Caymans, untouched. Carrizo's $50,000 was in the Swiss account, waiting for him to retrieve it at his leisure. She had changed out of her jeans and t-shirt, opting instead for a pair of khaki slacks and a light sweater for her meeting with Carrizo.

  The Range Rover stopped at the front door and Anne took a seat in the tower facing the elevator door while Carrizo exited the vehicle. He walked directly to the elevator and rode to the third floor, removing his blazer on the ride up. He draped the coat over his left arm and strolled into the tower. He walked directly to Anne, held out his hand to her and asked her if she would like a drink.

"A gin and tonic if you have it." Anne shook his hand and marveled that this renowned drug dealer, murderer, and corrupter of entire elections could be so civilized, could appear almost benign when he chose to. Taking a cue from Tru's playbook, Anne stood and looked the man in the eye. "Are you planning to kill us when this is over?"

Carrizo laughed out loud and gathered her hand into both of his. He patted her hand reassuringly and said "Dios Mio! No. NO! I have no desire to take your lives. To be honest I am beginning to find each of you fascinating. Well, perhaps not the Sheriff, he is essentially a blank page to me at this time."

Carrizo released her hand, carefully laid his jacket over the arm of her chair and walked briskly to the bar. He mixed a gin and tonic for each of them with a jaunty little slice of lime on each glass. "The limes come from my own orchards, you may find them slightly stronger than the generic versions in the grocery stores. Please sit, relax. You are in no danger here.""

Anne accepted the drink and sank into an arm chair across from the man and waited. "I must say, Mrs. Ramos, I am surprised to learn about your childhood. Bravo to you. You have made a life to be proud of. I hope the Sheriff appreciates you. Tell me…does he know about your ability to manipulate money around the globe?"

She squeezed the lime into her glass before responding, "No." She sighed and continued, "Jonathon has no idea yet. I did not want to distract him just yet."

"Hmmm. And the Marcus couple?" Carrizo sipped and crossed his legs.

"No. Sometimes it's better to let people assume I'm soft and quiet and not interested in certain things."" Anne pushed her feet out of her shoes and curled her legs under her in the chair. She figured she might as well relax and get comfortable.

"Hmmm." Carrizo was watching her closely. "Why charity donations? You could have done anything at all with the cash."

"I believe in those causes. Jonathon makes a reasonable living, but I've never been able to give more than a few hundred dollars a year to any of them." Carrizo nodded as he listened to Anne. He believed her, it WAS just that simple.

Carrizo stood and held his jacket open in front of him, reached into the interior pocket and produced a printed piece of paper. He handed it to Anne and regained his seat. She took it and gave him a questioning glance before she unfolded the page. Two columns of numbers, the first listing each of the donations she had made earlier in the day. The second column listed matching amounts to each charity. She stared at Jorge for several long moments without commenting, then said softly, "You matched each one? Why?"

Carrizo sipped his drink, then replied, "You earned it. You out maneuvered me. You actually took me by surprise and that is quite rare." He tipped his head her way and raised his glass to her. Anne raised her glass in acknowledgement and actually relaxed for real.

They watched the sun set in quiet conversation about books, movies, their children, and the news coming out of China about yet another new flu strain. Carrizo's housekeeper arrived and made them chicken mole from scratch. Carrizo held out a chair at the table for Anne as if she were an honored guest. They studiously avoided discussion of what might be happening out in the jungle.

Chapter 39

Hector was bent down behind the altar base when the Sheriff walked in. It was too dark to see anything clearly, but he could hear the man's familiar tread on the stones in front of the altar. He had no emotional attachment to Jonathon Ramos, but he hated having to kill him all the same. There would be no coming back from killing a respected Texas Sheriff, even if he was out of his jurisdiction. He listened and counted the steps as the Sheriff approached the table. When he could hear the man's breathing, Hector stood up smoothly and fired twice with less than twenty foot separating the two men. The Sheriff stumbled back with the first shot, fell to the ground with the second round and still managed to fire the shotgun once at Hector's back as he ran past.

Hector hit the tunnel again at a full run, four rounds left in his pistol, and the knowledge that Chris Marcus wouldn't be far behind. He stumbled once in the pitch black, bumping his knee on the stone wall as the tunnel came to a "T". He paused trying to work out which direction to go, turned left and the floor began to drop away in a sharp descent under his feet. He was forced to slow down and keep his left hand against the wall as he moved further downhill. The smooth stone floor gave way to steps so suddenly, he almost fell down them. Regaining his balance, he bent over with his hands on his knees and tried to catch his breath. He could hear noises behind him, but felt confident Chris Marcus would stop and help Sheriff Ramos, giving him a few precious minutes head start. He eased down the four steps and was relieved to find the tunnel picked up once again, allowing him to run. His left hand was still using the wall for support and guidance and now he could feel soft, moist patches of moss every few feet. The smell of bat guano was beginning to filter up to him as well. He coughed and tried to clear his nostrils, but did not stop his forward momentum.

Hector stumbled into a turn and a circular doorway. He stopped and listened. He could hear voices ahead of him in the dark, he had no idea who else was in the temple and he didn't care. Their presence meant there had to be another exit and he wasn't about to let them interfere with his escape. Hector slipped into the chamber and braced himself against the round doorframe with his pistol pointed in the general direction of the voices moving toward him. He held the flashlight in the other hand, off, but ready to use.

Viggo stopped suddenly in the tunnel and Tru ran right into the back of him, bounced off him and landed awkwardly on her sore ankle. ""Why are you sitting there?"

Viggo was staring back down at her and offered his hand to help her up. Tru took his giant paw and pulled herself upright. "Give me some warning when you stop like that. My ankle is weak from earlier.""

He merely grunted. There was a scraping noise ahead of them, like feet bracing. Viggo was certain Hector was still around or Chris would have been calling out for Tru. They crept forward a few more minutes before coming to a stop at a staircase leading up inside the temple. The odor of bats and something else, something old and spoiled floated all around their heads. There was something loose and hard rattling under their feet, making each step treacherous for Viggo and almost like skating for Tru's bad ankle. The lower stairs were covered in fallen pieces of rock and dirt that had been undisturbed for centuries. Tru pulled out her Blackberry and turned on the flashlight app to take a closer look.

"SHIT!" she gasped and pressed closer to Viggo as her light played over the floor and their feet. "JESUS GOD! What in the hell?" She was bouncing from foot to foot now, trying to find a way to just stand on air instead of the freak show on the floor.

"Be still. I cannot see what it is with the light floating everyvhere." Viggo's tone was even, but his accent was peeking out again. "I zink ve are standink on bones."

Tru cocked her head and hissed, "You zink? I'm pretty damn sure that is a SKULL on your boot!"

Viggo felt the hairs on the back of his neck stand up, but he spoke softly and moved calmly toward the staircase. "Mrs. Marcus. Follow me, ve vill take ze stairs and zen get out of here." He tapped her with his elbow and she linked her arm through it, still holding the Blackberry. It's light bounced as they tottered to the steps. Once they were on the fourth step up, they turned and Tru shined the light across the entire floor of the room they had crossed. It was full of white and grey bones, femurs, arm bones, collar bones, rib cages and skulls. Every inch of the floor was layered in either whole bones or the powder of those that had long since disintegrated.

"I hate the Mayans." they spoke at the same time and stared at each other. Tru gave a whole body shudder of disgust and backed up the next two steps, light still playing out on the unburied before them. Viggo turned his back to the room and said "I vill lead and you hold onto my shirt behind. OK?"

They reached the top of the stairs and found a round, rolling door half blocking the entrance to the temple. There was room to pass one at a time into what was a very large chamber with no light of any sort yet again. Tru had just reached for her phone when Viggo stilled her hand and leaned very close to her head. "Nyet. No light, listen."

Tru un-holstered her Glock and held it loosely in her right hand. They could hear running feet coming from a distance to the right and a the closer sounds of a man breathing heavily. Suddenly a flash of light half blinded them as Hector's flashlight beam bounced in front of him and he barreled into the chamber a hundred feet from where they stood. Viggo brought his shotgun up and fired. The flashlight fell to the ground and two more shots rang out, leaving all three of them temporarily deafened. The second shot no sooner registered in Tru's ears than Viggo collapsed to the ground at her feet in a giant pile. Tru did not hesitate, she stepped over Viggo's prone form and fired four rounds one after the other in a sweeping motion. She knelt down on her left knee in front of Viggo, sparing her weak ankle and fired another two shots at the oval lens of the flash light. The bulb exploded with the second round. She had one bullet left in the chamber and another full magazine in her pocket.

Tru was blind and deaf from the gunfire, but she was thinking clearly and knew Hector would be at the same disadvantage. She had no idea if she had hit Hector or not and she had no way of moving Viggo's enormous mass. So she laid on the ground in front of him, grabbed the second magazine from her pocket, ejected the empty one and inserted the full one. She breathed through her nose, the burnt smell of gunpowder overpowered the hint of rot and mold that the temple exuded. Tru waited five long minutes for her hearing to begin to return, she spent the entire time in front of Viggo, determined to protect him from further harm if at all possible. She was afraid to touch him, if he were dead, she did not want to know.

Chris scooted across the altar alcove to the Sheriff's side. Jonathon was sitting up with his back against the base of the sacrifice table. He was gasping for air and clutching his chest with one hand. ""I don't think I hit the son of a bitch Chris."

"I'm pretty sure he got you. Can you feel your legs? I need to get you out of here." Chris ran his fingers around the Sheriff's belt, feeling for his Maglite.

"One direct shot to the chest." Jonathon was huffing with each word. "One graze to the hip. That one"s going to make walking impossible." He coughed and sweat dripped off his forehead, leaving wet droplets on the stone floor between his legs.

Chris closed his eyes for a moment, trying to take it all in. "Let me get this light going and we'll see what we see. I don't want to carry your tall ass all the way back to the truck. And I am NOT taking you home to Anne if you're dead."

"Vest. Vest took the chest hit. Took my wind." More coughing. Chris handed the light to Jonathon and he pointed it at his own chest while Chris tore open his shirt over the armored vest. He breathed a sigh of relief at the single hole in the center near the breast bone, the bullet clearly visible. The hip wound was bleeding freely, a clean hole through the pant leg, in the fleshy part of the hip and out the backside of the man's right buttock. Chris let out a low whistle and helped Jonathon take his shirt of. He folded it into a tight square and tucked it under the Sheriff's exit wound, then he took off his own t-shirt and padded the hip the same way.

"Just sit tight. I'll come back for you." Chris stood back up, double checked his own weapons and headed back into the tunnel. He needed to find Hector and finish this once and for all.

Chris had just run down the four steps that almost tripped Hector when he heard gunfire somewhere below. The shots echoed up the passage, flowed over Chris like a wave. He wasn't positive, but he thought he heard the same pistol earlier when Hector shot the Sheriff and this time another handgun and definitely a shotgun. He poured on the speed and careened down the tunnel with his own shotgun held in front of him ready to fire. He skidded through the curve and had to duck his head a swarm of bats came out of the chamber ahead. Their odor almost overwhelmed him and he was forced to lie flat on the floor to avoid being pummeled as hundreds of Mexican brown bats filled the tunnel. Chris hated, truly hated three things in the world and one of those was bats. They scared the bejeesus out of him, creeped him out in a way that nothing else did. Once the swarm was gone, he stood up and flattened himself against the round doorway, heart thudding and eyes straining to see anything more than shadows. He could hear ragged breathing close to him, maybe ten feet away and what sounded like whispered voices further into the chamber.

Chris reached into his pocket and found his cell phone, he hoped like Hell Tru had ignored him and put a flashlight app on his phone. He was technologically stubborn and normally refused to use his phone for anything other than actual calls. Tru had every gadget known to man and spent many a happy hour updating, upgrading and up-spending said gadgets. He found the icon and a narrow beam of light shot out in front of him, highlighting Hector laying in a fetal position on the filthy floor just inside the entry. Chris waved the light back and forth over Hector, but remained behind the cover of the wall and hollered, ""Trudy? Honey? You in there?"

"I'm here, got Viggo with me. He"s down." The relief in her voice was obvious. "Are you ok?"

"I'm fine. Hector shot Jonathon, he had his vest on." Chris reached down and kicked Hector's foot. The man groaned, rolled over and began to raise his pistol in Chris' direction. Chris instantly pulled the trigger and the sound of the shotgun drown everything else out. Hector's skull exploded and grey-white brain matter mixed with the blood that had already been running from his upper left shoulder and back. Hector's entire body went limp and still, his pistol slid out of his dead fingers against the stone floor. Chris waited a moment for his ears to clear before yelling out to Tru, "Were you the one who got Hector in the shoulder or Viggo?"

Tru's reply was matter of fact, "Not sure. Viggo got off one shot and I got out four or five."

Chris bent down and inspected the wound more closely with the light from his phone. "Looks like a .45 hole. Way to go baby." He pocketed Hector's pistol before standing up and shining his light into the cavernous room.

"Is he dead?" Tru sounded like she was carrying a heavy weight.

"You might ought to work on your aim, I had to finish him." Chris had his business as usual voice on. "I"m heading over to you now."

Tru was still laying on the ground, listening to Hector moan in the dark when Chris' light appeared in the entry. She brought her Glock up and aimed for the open doorway until she heard Chris' voice calling her name. The sense of relief was so great, she felt dizzy and her hands trembled when she lowered her weapon. She sat up and flinched when Chris shot Hector in the head, the sound reverberating through the chamber. While she spoke to her husband, Tru perched on her knees and leaned over Viggo"s face to see if he still breathed. She tried to lift his upper half up and slapped his face.

Viggo spoke so suddenly Tru almost dropped his head to the stone floor. "I was just beginning to like you and now you are slapping me."

Tru giggled, she couldn't help it, the adrenaline and fear and relief all combined to spew out in ridiculous, irrational, girly laughter. Even Viggo grinned at her as Chris reached them and knelt down beside his wife. Chris swept her into a huge bear hug and kissed the top of her head.

"Ugh. You're wet." He pushed her back slightly and shined his phone light over her and then Viggo. "Where are you hit big man? Can you stand?"

Viggo pushed himself to a sitting position and ran his hands over his body. "Sheriff Ramos isn't the only one here wearing armor." Chris and Tru both shined their phone lights on Viggo and he pulled his shirt up to his chin. Beneath was a thin, super light armored vest with a bullet wedged in just above his belly button. He was bleeding from the temple and a pretty ugly cut on his forearm, but no bullet wounds. "I doubled over when I was hit, slammed my head into the wall and was out for several seconds. I will live."

Tru harrumphed loudly and both men looked her way. "You were only out for a few seconds. And you just laid there like a big dead fucking lump? YOU SCARED ME TO DEATH!" She reached over and thumped him in the forehead with her middle finger.

Viggo snatched her hand out of the air and held it lightly. "I could not shoot back without endangering you after you leapt over me. When you laid down, I planned to use your body as a brace for my shotgun, but you swapped magazines and seemed to have your quarry penned down." He released her hand and waited to see if she was going to tweak his nose next.

"Ummm….boys and girls….. I hate to interrupt your lover's spat here, but we've got shit to do." Chris taunted them and held out a hand to help Viggo to his feet. "Damn son, you weigh as much as one of our draft horses!" Both men grunted as Viggo regained his footing.

The three of them walked to Hector's prone body and stood there for a moment. Viggo silently recrossed the room and picked up his forgotten machete.

"Chris, where is your shirt?" Tru had just noticed her husband's lovely bare chest.

"Bandage." Chris looked down in disgust at what was left of Hector, then he met Viggo's stare. "We can't leave him here. Give me your shirt."

Viggo said nothing, just pulled his t-shirt over his head and helped Chris wrap it around the stump where Hector's head had been intact four minutes earlier. The two men lifted him up between them and proceeded to drag his body back into the main tunnel, a trail of blood following. Tru lead the way with her phone light. The bats were long gone, but it took almost fifteen minutes to maneuver their way back to the altar room where Sheriff Ramos waited.

The men dropped Hector's body and Chris followed Tru to Jonathon's side. Viggo stayed next to Hector and searched the man's pockets. Jonathon declined Tru's offer to assess his wounds, saying he would rather just die first, thank you. Viggo chuckled and said, ""I know how you feel."

"MEN. Jonathon I don't want to feel your ass, I just want to make sure you're not bleeding to death there." Tru would never understand male pride. "If you think you"re healthy enough, can we get out of this tomb?"

Tru flashed her dimming Blackberry toward the exit and moved into the hall. Chris helped the Sheriff to his feet and supported half his weight telling Tru which way to go. Viggo stretched and popped his knuckles before he reached down and dragged Hector over his shoulder in a fireman's carry. Tru glanced back and pointed a finger at Viggo with a grin, "SEE? Gorilla."

"Mr. Marcus?" Viggo spoke as if Hector weighed no more than a bag of groceries.

Chris was under a bit more strain. 'What?'"

"Sooner or later, one of us has to explain to your wife what cartel enforcer actually means."

"She knows Viggo. She just doesn't care anymore. Apparently my wife likes you." This drew actual laughter from the Sheriff, followed by a round of coughing.

When his hacking subsided, the Sheriff piped in, ""Watch out Viggo. Tru and Anne will have you on the Christmas card lists.""

"I hate dealing with women." Viggo muttered softly so Tru wouldn't hear him up ahead. "Turn here, swim in this hole, walk on these dead people, drag this moron around. It is always something!"

"WHAT IS ALL THAT LAUGHTER BACK THERE? Two of you are gunshot, one of you is dead and you're cackling like a bunch of hyenas." Tru was waiting for them at the mud encased steps leading back to the world.

The entrance almost glowed in the post storm sunshine. The humidity slammed into Tru like a speeding train, sucking the very breath from her lungs. Tru darted ahead and drove the Defender up to the cordon blocking the dig steps from public access. She backed up to the very edge of the first step and opened the back door. Viggo stomped up and flung Hector's body into the back, making sure to tuck the legs and curl the body up so it fit properly. Then he went back down the steps to help Chris and the Sheriff up. Sheriff Ramos laid on his left side in the second row, huffing and puffing, looking very pale. The back of his pants down to the ankle was covered in blood and mud and sweat was beading on his forehead. Tru found a bottle of water under the seat and offered to the man with two ibuprofen from the glove box.

Viggo nodded at Chris and said "Go to the Celestun house. We'll be behind you in my truck. I'll handle the body later, but Sheriff Ramos needs a doctor."

Chris shook hands with Viggo, kissed his wife on the mouth and drove away. Tru and Viggo followed minutes later in the Nissan truck.

Chapter 40

They were finishing a warm cherry tart and debating the merits of an ivy league education in England versus one in the United States when the GPS alarm pinged on Carrizo's phone. He picked it up and smiled at Anne over the table. "They are on the move again." He passed her the phone and Anne eyed the map for a full minute laying it back on the table.

Carrizo stood and held his elbow out to Anne, ""Do you play chess?"

Anne smiled as she stood and said, "It seems certain that you already know the answer to that." They retired to Carrizo's study and he brought out a custom chess set. Each piece was made of hand shaped and hammered copper, trimmed in silver or gold, and the board was carved marble and teak wood. Six moves and Anne was bringing out her bishop when Carrizo's phone rang.

He looked at the screen, begged her indulgence for the interruption and answered the phone. "Viggo. Has your day been productive?" A pause. "In the catacombs of a temple? Truly?" A longer pause and then Carrizo stood up and walked to his desk. "How many shots?" He listened and opened the middle drawer of the desk. "You as well? Everything you need will be waiting for your arrival. And Viggo? Well done." Carrizo disconnected the call, pushed a button in the drawer and retook his seat at the chess board.

Within moments the chauffer appeared in the study door. Carrizo issued orders in a crisp manner and moved to sit next to Anne. "We will need a doctor on the premises in 15 minutes. At least two gunshot wounds, a head trauma and broken ribs. Also, have the housekeeper bring two mugs of café au lait and then send her home. Before the doctor arrives." The chauffer vanished without a question. Five minutes later Carrizo had explained the incoming situation to Anne and then she was holding a steaming mug of foamy coffee and milk. Anne drank a quarter of it, relishing the burn against the roof of her mouth. The pain helped clear her head and narrow her focus. Part of her wanted to run sobbing to the driveway so she could see her husband immediately, but the nurse in her knew better. Let them get him in the house calmly and she could assess his medical needs like a professional.

By the time the Land Rover passed through the gate, the doctor was already setting up in one of the bedrooms. He had brought a portable field surgery kit and a small pharmacy of medications, iv drips, heart monitor and his own nurse. Chris and the chauffer came inside with the Sheriff supported between them. He was pale and weak, but took the time to kiss Anne on the forehead before they laid him down on the bed. The doctor immediately began to remove Jonathon's clothes and the vest with the bullet embedded in it. Anne stood beside Jonathon, holding his hand as the wounds were revealed. The vest had stopped the bullet in his chest, but left a huge, ugly bruise and three broken ribs. The doctor's concern was primarily for his hip, but broken ribs can lead to punctured lungs, so they were being very careful.

Chris stepped out and gave them room to work. Carrizo touched him on the shoulder silently and gestured for Chris to follow him into the study. Once inside, Carrizo closed the door and offered Chris a cup of coffee from the urn the housekeeper had fixed before she left.

"Where is my wife?" Chris was curt, but he took the coffee.

"She and Viggo are enroute now." Carrizo took a seat on the leather sofa next to the fireplace. "Would you care to clean up before they arrive?"

Chris glanced down at himself briefly and

remembered that he had no shirt on, his pants were layered in grime and blood and his boots were no better. He had tracked mud onto what appeared to be

a very expensive Persian rug. He shrugged and sat down on the sofa with Carrizo, sipping his coffee. ""I think I'll wait for Tru."

"As you wish. Can I have my driver fix you a meal while we wait?"

"Jesus. You are something else. My friend has been shot, my wife is out there with your hired killer, who was shot as well by the way, there's a dead man in the back of the car, I feel like I have been trampled by donkeys and here you are. Like I've dropped in for lunch without calling ahead first." Chris was through caring if Carrizo took offense or not.

Carrizo stifled the twitch under his eye, offered an almost invisible nod of his head and said quietly, "I do not take these things lightly. I simply see no reason for your wife to assume the worst when she arrives to find you no better off than when you left the ruins."

Chris said nothing. Instead he leaned back on the sofa, stretched his legs out to rest on the coffee table and savored his coffee. Technology wasn't the only thing he was stubborn about. Being told how to treat his wife by another man just made him dig in his heels.

Carrizo's phone buzzed with a text message from the gate guard, preventing an escalation of male machismo that neither would win. "And here they are now."

Both men stood as Viggo and Tru entered the room. Tru was first and ran to Chris. She kissed him and then stood back, casting a critical eye over his bare chest and filthy pants. "What? You forgot to pack a clean shirt?"

Carrizo roared with laughter and clapped Chris on the back before saying, "I tried to warn you."

Chris narrowed his eyes at his wife and asked what had taken them so long. Viggo cleared his throat and everyone looked his way. ""I had to go back into the catacombs and retrieve everyone's bullet casings. I saw no point in leaving unnecessary, obvious signs of our presence.""

Chris groaned, "I can't believe I forgot something so basic as picking up my brass. Thanks Viggo." He shook the big man's hand.

"This is my profession, Mr. Marcus. It"s what I do. Senor Carrizo… I do have the small matter of trash disposal."

Carrizo grimaced briefly and walked to the study door with a hand on Viggo's arm. "My friend, I think you will see the doctor first. Your entire scalp is covered in dried blood." They walked directly to the bedroom where the Sheriff was being treated.

Tru and Chris went through the kitchen on their way to their bedroom, Tru needed a Dr Pepper. Once in the privacy of the bedroom, they sank onto the bed together and snuggled in silence. An hour passed before either one realized they had been sleeping. Anne's knock on the door brought them back to the present. Tru ran to let her in.

"Jonathon is fine. He's sedated heavily. I wanted him to sleep. A few broken ribs, but the hip wound was clean. In and out. No broken bone and no bullet fragmentation either." Her relief was visible. "I don't know all of what happened down there Chris, but it sounds like you probably saved Jonathon's life and I won't forget that." Tru wrapped her arms around Anne.

"I know we were just acquaintances before, but we're family now. You don't owe Chris anything at all. NOTHING." Chris was nodding in agreement from the bed with a big smile on his face.

Anne grinned back and said, "You know what this makes you, don't you?"

Tru cocked and eyebrow and stepped back, "What?"

"Big Damn Heroes."

"OH MY GOD! Chris! Anne's a Firefly fan! WHO KNEW?" Tru was utterly delighted. She was a huge sci-fi geek and Firefly was the comfort food of television in their house. Chris groaned with good humor.

"I have to get back to Jonathon and I think Viggo is looking for Chris." Anne closed the bedroom door behind her softly and jogged back downstairs.

Chris got up and took a five minute shower as only a man can do. Tru got in the water just as he stepped out and her version of the five minute shower was more along the lines of twelve minutes. Chris banged on the shower door and hollered, "Honey! Hurry up or we're leaving you here."

"I'm coming. Good grief. You don"t seriously think I'm not going to shave my legs do you?"

Chris rolled his eyes and muttered all the way out of the bathroom, down the hall, and into the kitchen where Viggo and Carrizo were seated with fresh coffee. Viggo glanced at him as he pulled a cup out of the cabinet and couldn't suppress a grin. "Mrs. Marcus?"

Chris rested his head against the cabinet door and said, "Of course. She's a woman isn't she?"

All three men shared a knowing look and Carrizo pushed the coffee pot toward Chris and a platter of left over cherry tart with drizzled icing. "We

have been discussing the best way to take out our leftover garbage."

Chris nodded and served himself a piece of the tart while he waited for Carrizo to continue. Carrizo looked very much like a man at his ease, perched on a kitchen stool, with a cup of coffee. He was in his shirt sleeves with the collar open and had changed to a pair of designer jeans and boat shoes. "I have no interest in the sail boat. If you would care to keep it, I can certainly arrange that. I had thought to make a gift of it to our good Sheriff. Alas, he finds the idea repugnant."

Chris shook his head, "I don't want it. We don't sail."

Tru presented herself at that moment, clean with freshly dried hair bouncing past her shoulders. "My dear!

You look much refreshed. I had no idea your hair was the color of fire. Muy bonito." Carrizo stood and offered her his seat. Viggo stood as well, Carrizo insisted on impeccable behavior in his presence.

"Thank you." She took his stool and Viggo raised an eyebrow. Carrizo simply pulled another one up for himself. ""Are you talking about giving Hector's boat to the Ramoses?" Tru accepted the Dr Pepper Chris pulled from the refrigerator for her. She inhaled deeply and turned to stare at Carrizo directly.

"Is that chicken mole I smell?"

"I believe a serving or two remains. Look in the oven ." Carrizo found constantly amused by this woman. In another situation that might have been dangerous for her, but right now, with these people, he relaxed and enjoyed the company.

Tru pulled out three containers out of the oven piled high with chicken, roasted potatoes, refried beans, Spanish rice, a bowl of jalepeno and tomatillo based salso, and a bowl of green beans of all things. Fresh corn tortillas were sitting in a little covered bowl in the microwave. Tru had an exaggerated Southern Belle moment - the back of her hand resting on her forehead, eyes batting, other hand fanning her face. In her best Scarlett O'Hara voice she cooed, "Why Jorge! You always amaze… All this food for little ol" me? I may need my smellin' salts?"

Viggo barked with laughter. Chris just drank his coffee, he had seen Tru's "Gone with the Wind" act before and he wasn't to the point of considering these people friends just yet. Carrizo pulled a stack of plates from a cabinet and suggested they make one up for the Sheriff. "When he comes out of that coma Anne put him in, he'll be very hungry."

They sat at the kitchen table while Tru scarfed enough food for two men. Viggo watched her eat with a mix of awe and horror. She"s wasn't a slob, just starving and she loved homemade Mexican food of any kind. Chris made a pair of burritos out of tortillas and some chicken. He paid no attention to Tru, he had been watching her eat for fifteen years. He looked up at Viggo's wide eyed stare and casually said, "You're wondering why she doesn't weigh 300lbs, right?"

Viggo nodded wordlessly and Carrizo answered, ""It's metabolism and working with horses all day."

Tru swallowed and pointed at Carrizo. "I"ve been meaning to ask you about your horses. Chris said you have an outstanding Andalusian stallion at the mountain camp."

Carrizo smiled, a true, open smile from the heart. He spread his hands and said, "I am a lover of fine things. My family had been breeding Spanish horses for literally hundreds of years. We show and sell them of course, but the best ones come home and stay in our private bloodlines. Our family stud book dates back to the 1600's in Spain. In fact, I have been doing a bit of research on your bloodlines the past few days."

Chris perked up now. "Then you know we have ancient genetics in our own horses. And three National and International champions in multiple disciplines."

Carrizo accepted the coffee refill Viggo offered, folded a tortilla and dipped it in the salsa before he replied. "I do. I also know that Trudy's little blue stallion can be traced back to three of my family's lines. It would seem we are family, after a fashion."

Chris snorted and looked at Tru. Tru shrugged and said, "I know." Viggo was silent, but he tensed slightly. He felt certain these people were at a cross roads. Choose one path and an alliance would be formed. Take the other and at some point in the future, Viggo be under orders to assure they either vanished or were compelled to remain silent forever. Chess with Carrizo was always a treacherous game, especially when the man was happy.

"Actually, I think your bloodlines run through a third of our mares." Tru pushed her plate away and wiped her mouth with her napkin. "I out-crossed a few years ago to refine the bone structure in our Spanish Normans. It worked well too."

Carrizo was relaxed, leaning back in his chair, legs crossed. He glanced at Viggo briefly, noting the big man's tension level. "Relax Viggo." His tone was soft and Viggo knew the right choice had been made. He would have hated to kill them. The truth was Viggo liked Tru and respected Chris for many reasons.

"Now. Business. I believe I have mentioned once before my distaste for loose ends." Carrizo nodded at Viggo and he took over the conversation.

"Disposal of the boat and Hector. Mrs. Marcus's presence is not required, but I do need someone in a second boat for the return trip." Viggo was matter of fact.

They could have been planning a camping trip for all he cared.

"Works for me. I'm ready now. Let"s get it done." Chris was already walking out of the room. Tru didn't move, she didn't really want to spend any more time with the dead Hector, but she wasn't about to be left out at the very end.

"Excuse me." Tru was peeved. ""You are not actuallyleaving me behind?"

Chris turned around and sighed. "Honey. For once will you just do what I ask? JUST ONCE?" He rubbed the bridge of his nose between his thumb and forefinger.

"Yeah…that's not going to happen. You're going to need a lookout or something. And honestly, Viggo doesn't swim all that well."

Viggo glared at her. "I was carrying a machete and a shotgun. Swimming a tunnel better suited to a midget."

"And you would be dead now if it weren"t for me." Tru retorted, but there was no hostility behind her words. "You need me."

Viggo excused himself to Carrizo, walked to Chris and said softly, "We can win this argument, but at what cost?" Viggo glanced back at Tru and continued, "Or I could just wring her neck. A personal favor to you. It would save you a great deal of trouble in the future.""

"I appreciate the offer Viggo, but I would like to resume my sex life at some point." Chris held out a hand out to Tru. "If you're coming, let's go."

Tru winked at Carrizo as she left the table. Ten minutes later all three of them were in the Land Rover once again. Hector's body had been rolled into a black tarp and the second row seats had been wiped clean of the Sheriff's blood. They drove to the Progreso marina mostly in silence.

Chapter 41

Chris dropped Viggo at the Libertad's dock, then drove a few miles further down the highway to Carrizo's private dock. The night watchman met them at the gate, he was expecting them. He opened the gate and they were able to drive directly onto the dock to a fishing boat. Chris and Tru wrestled with the body and the tarp until they got it out of the vehicle and onto the boat deck. It had been long enough for rigor mortis to begin to set up.

Tru untied the boat from it's moorings while Chris warmed the engine and tried to make sense of the charts in the bridge. Once they were free to go, he eased the trawler away from the dock and out into the night sea. Almost an hour passed before they saw the mast of the Libertad ahead, waiting for them.

Viggo had to plug the diesel line hole and add three quarts of oil before the engine would even start. He poured diesel out of a five gallon can from the storage room, the entire tank had leaked during the day. He had a moment to envision himself repairing the engine with popsicle sticks and bubble-gum while Tru said "told you so" over his shoulder. Viggo said a prayer that the thing did not go up in flames from the fumes. Fortunately, luck was with him. He waited until he saw no one on the dock or near enough to identify which boat was leaving before he pulled away. The water was calm, the morning's storm long since gone. Viggo used the motor and left the sails rolled, it was a short trip and the sooner they were done, the better.

He dropped anchor in the empty ocean and listened to the water gently slapping the sides of the Libertad while he waited for Chris and Tru. The inky blackness of the night split and revealed the fishing boat with a single light at the bow and one on the bridge. Viggo sat on the deck of the Libertad, eating a piece of sharp cheddar cheese from the pantry as they approached, washing it down with a Tecate beer. He rarely drank, but it had been one of those days.

Chris maneuvered the fishing boat to within fifteen feet of the Libertad and Tru tossed a catch rope at Viggo. He reached up and caught it in one hand before standing back up. Once the two boats were tied together, Chris and Tru hauled the trawler as close as possible and Viggo redid the knots, keeping them side by side. He held out his hand to Tru. She took it and jumped onto the Libertad. "Thank you good sir."

Viggo crossed onto the fishing boat with Chris. The two of them hefted Hector's corpse between them and tossed him like a bag of grain across the water to the Libertad's deck. Tru bounced back out of the way and shuddered. She put aside her revulsion and bent down to untie the tarp so the boys could roll the body out.

It took all three of them to drag Hector down into the cabin. Tru went directly back topside and gulped fresh salt air. The last thing she wanted to do was throw up in front of Chris and Viggo. She would never hear the end of it.

"How are we going to sink this bitch?"" Chris wiped the sweat from his brow and looked around the tiny cabin.

Viggo grinned and said, "Come look. I had some time on the boat before you flushed the rat at the fish shack." He bent down and lifted the engine room trapdoor. The underside had a small lump of grey clay like material stuck there with several wires and a digital timer blinking all zeros.

Chris whistled and eyed Viggo with a new respect. ""You're just full of tricks, aren't you? Where were you before Carrizo hired you?"

"Around. Some work with the French, the Saudis, that sort of thing." Viggo bent to the bomb and verified the connections were still correct and intact.

"Why go private for Carrizo?"

"I wanted to slow down. See the world from a private plane instead of hiding in the cargo hold." Viggo closed the trapdoor and stood up again. "Are you ready?"

"More than ready. I could use a nap and some downtime with my wife." Chris led the way to the ladder out of the cabin.

Viggo chuckled. Chris looked back at him and said, "Tru will drive you crazy, but it's always worth it.""

Viggo shook his head and said, "Somehow I don't envy you. Wait a second. Want a laugh?"

Chris stepped off the ladder and listened to what Viggo had in mind. They both snickered when he was finished and made their way back topside where Tru waited.

She was pacing the deck and turned at the sounds of them shutting the cabin door behind them. "What took you so long? Can we GO already? It's just too damn creepy out here with a dead guy and the water and all this… silence."

Chris bent to untie the knots holding the boats together, Viggo bounced from the Libertad to the fishing boat and held out his hand for Tru again. Once all three of them were off the Libertad and the ropes coiled back in place, Chris went to the bridge and started the engines. "Hey boys? What about the sail boat?"

Chris shrugged and said "It's a slow leak. The water will fill it slowly and she'll just sink." He had to turn away before Tru saw the glimmer in his eye.

They had been moving for ten minutes, the Libertad was still in view, but already retreating. Viggo leaned on the deck rail next to Tru and pulled his phone out of his pocket. He handed it to her and said ""Senor Carrizo requested that you call him when we had completed our task.""

"You call him. He's your boss."" Tru held the phone without glancing at it.

Viggo held his hands in the air, shaking his head, "Nyet. He asked that you let him know. Just press the green button and the call will go through."

Chris had moved to the bridge door, behind his wife and was stifling laughter. Tru gave a put upon sigh, put her thumb to the green button and pressed it. The explosion was magnificent. Orange, yellow, and red flames and fireballs shot into the sky like fireworks. A wall of flame encircled the Libertad and shot out over the water like a living thing. The enormous sound swept over them like a flood.

Viggo stared at Tru with a look of horror and shouted, "VAT DID YOU DO? VAT DID YOU DO? I told you to push ze GREEN button! Oh my Gott! You blew it up. Vhy?"

Tru flung his phone to the deck, slowly stepping back and away from the Russian and his crazy eyes. She stuttered, "I…I…I did hit the green one. I did, you saw me push the green button. I swear!"

Chris was laughing so hard he was doubled over and finally had to sit all the way on the floor, tears streaming down his face, hiccups overwhelming him. Tru whirled on him and froze while he and Viggo cackled and blustered and slapped their legs. The Libertad burned behind them, slowly succumbing to the ocean's pull.

"You rotten, filthy, evil, sexist pigs!"" Tru retrieved Viggo's cell phone and flung it at his head. It bounced off his huge chest and he just laughed harder. Chris was laying on his side in the bridge doorway, hysterical. "I swear to God! Chris if you EVER want to have sex again, you will shut up NOW."

Viggo waved his hand and tried to speak, but couldn't. Tru looked from one to the other and said, "Are you crying? Viggo…are YOU CRYING?" That broke her and she bent over the rail in breathless gales of her own laughter. They went directly back to Celestun, rather than returning to Progreso. Carrizo could send someone else for the Defender later. The trip took two hours and they laughed the entire way.

Anne and the Sheriff were both awake when the threesome returned to the house. They paid the taxi at the gate and walked thto the house. Carrizo and Anne were sitting in arm chairs at the foot of the Sheriff's bed. Tru took the last chair in the room while Chris and Viggo lurked near the doorway.

"Excellent! We are all together once again. The three of you look none the worse for wear." Carrizo eyed each one carefully. He raised an eyebrow at Viggo's good humor. The big man was still snickering now and then when he thought about the look on Tru's face during the explosion.

"Yes, sir. All went according to plan. The trash has been incinerated." Viggo and Chris both starting laughing again, eyes closed and sides shaking.

"SHUT IT! You insufferable swine!" Tru was trying her hardest to be disgusted and put out, but it was hard to take her seriously when she was starting to giggle again.

Anne was starting now and she didn't even know why they were all laughing. "What is going on?" Chris was the first to regain control and he shared the gag with the rest of the room. Even the Sheriff giggled, full laughter hurt his ribs too much.

"Chris, son, that might have been a mistake." Jonathon scooted up a bit against the headboard, "A woman scorned and all…."

Tru eyed Viggo until he stood perfectly still and met her gaze. "You will find out that you don't have to be married to me to face my wrath. I WILL get you. In public. When you least expect it."" She flounced out of the room, even Carrizo was laughing as she left.

Carrizo grinned and said, "I realize you are all tired and apparently, punch drunk." He nodded at Tru's exit. "However, there are still some loose ends to address. I apologize, but I must insist we finalize our situation tonight. I have to be in London tomorrow night and I really must return to my home tonight."

Chris and the Sheriff nodded, Anne held up a hand and said, "I need to tell you something. TRU! Come back." Tru was lurking in the hallway and appeared almost immediately. Anne continued, "Jorge, your $50,000 is in this Swiss account. The access information is on this piece of paper." Anne pulled a scrap of paper out of her pocket and handed it to him.

"Thank you." Carrizo put it in his own pocket without even glancing at it.

"Anne? Who moved the money?" Jonathon was looking at his wife.

"I did. I did not want Hector to get his hands on it again." She shrugged her shoulders, looked at Jonathon and sat on the foot of the bed. "You can do what you want with it. It's sitting in a different account in the Cayman Islands."

"That reminds me!" Tru jumped into the silence as fast she could. "Hector's duffle bag was in the Defender. Did anyone think to get it out?"

Viggo nodded and said, "I brought it inside when I rolled Hector in the tarp. It's in the gun safe. Along with the money I found in his pockets at the ruins."

Carrizo stood and said nothing, merely waited for everyone to look his way. When he had the room's attention, he spoke. "Excellent. As always Viggo. Now, I have had my people handling the paper trail Hector left behind. As far as they can tell, the Sheriff's connection has been erased. Sheriff Ramos, I will leave it to you to explain Hector's absence, it is no longer my concern. I have no interest in destroying your career, the money Hector left behind is yours to keep or dispose of as you see fit." He walked to the doorway and paused, looking at Tru. "I would very much like to talk horses with you. I have a young colt that might interest you.""

Carrizo was gone. Mere minutes later he and Viggo were in the Range Rover heading back to the airport. Everyone was quiet, the house actually seemed to have gone to sleep with Carrizo's departure. It was if they were in the aftermath of a tornado.

Chris broke the silence first. "Jonathon, I know you said you don't want Hector's money, but I think that's a mistake. I may have a way for you to keep it and your pension. If you're interested?"

"I'm listening." Jonathon could feel Anne's eyes on him, but he refused to look at her yet.

"You know I run a small consulting firm and I do business all over the world. I am always on the lookout for men like you. Experienced, calm, capable of handling a bad situation without getting carried away." Tru was nodding in agreement. "Finish your term with the county.

I'll move that money into a couple of our business accounts. Just let it sit there. When you retire, if you want, I'll pay you a substantial hiring bonus. Come work for me."

Tru was thrilled. She knew Chris would figure something out, it was what he did best. Anne was nodding now as she digested the offer. Jonathon said nothing for a long time. Finally he sighed and said, "Can I think about it? Couple of weeks maybe?"

Chris held out his hand and they shook solemnly.

Chapter 42

It had been two weeks since the Yucatan business and Tru was staring at the letter she had just opened. Chris ambled into their kitchen and walked up behind her. He kissed the side of her neck before he asked, ""Whatcha' reading?"

"Apparently the entire $18,000 hospital bill from Alpine has been paid in full. This is a receipt for our records." Tru turned halfway around and looked up at Chris. "Did you take money from the IRA and pay it?"

"Nope. You told me to send them $2000 a month and let the cash earn what little interest it could. I just wrote the first check this morning for tomorrow's mail actually."

They stared at the receipt with it's big red "PAID" stamp and then their eyes met. "Carrizo"" both said at once.

Chris rolled his eyes and said "Should have known it. He likes to show off whenever possible."

Tru nodded and thought about it for a minute before replying, "Works for me. Did you talk to the Ramoses? Are they going to meet us in New Orleans for Thanksgiving?"

"Yes and yes. Jonathon said he would prefer it if we did not vacation in his jurisdiction again for at least six months. Something about letting sleeping dogs lie."

"Can you blame him? If we stay away, Carrizo will stay away and he gets out of this clean. Has he given you an answer about the job offer?" Tru hugged Chris and looked up at him until he kissed her lips.

"No and we are NOT going to pester him. Are you?"

"When we get to New Orleans, I want to ask Anne what she did with her time while we were down in the ruins. I noticed her laptop was in Carrizo's study when we got back. What do you think the two of them were doing?"

Chris took her chin in his fingers and begged his wife, "Tru. Trudy. Please, for God's sake, just this once will you do as I ask and leave it alone? Just once."

The End

All characters in this book are fictional and do not exist. Any similarity in name or personality to living persons is entirely coincidental and unintentional. While geographical locations and or products or actual business may be real, they have been fictionalized for the purposes of telling this fictional story. Additionally, the author has taken some liberites with exact geographical locations and distances for the purposes of literary expediency.

Cover art is original artwork by the artist, Jeran Walker. The paintings are of actual locations in the Big Bend area of West Texas. Originals can be purchased by visiting the artist's website at jerart.com

The author lives with Rhodesian Ridgeback dogs, several Spanish Mustang and Spanish Norman horses in deep East Texas and has spent many happy years living in the Big Bend area of Texas. Sadly, the author is just too darn poor to own a helicopter or private plane and must resort to driving around the Yucatan on vacation.